One Small Step

It's the crime of the century—but not this century. And there are two hundred and twenty-seven million witnesses—but none of them can help the investigating officers.

For this is murder on the moon in the year 2010. And when Emile Lemarque keels over on the steps of the space ship *Europa*, he stirs up more than lunar dust as his death threatens to turn into an international incident, requiring the personal intervention of Commissioner Peter Pascoe of the Eurofed Justice Department.

Pascoe, at the peak of his career and facing one of his most baffling and delicate cases, turns for assistance to his old mentor, Andy Dalziel, now deep in gouty retirement. Reunited, though with roles reversed, the old Mid-Yorkshire duo probe deep into space, both inner and outer, as they take one small step after another to a series of surprising truths.

REGINALD HILL

One Small Step

A Dalziel and Pascoe novella

COLLINS, 8 GRAFTON STREET, LONDON W1

William Collins Sons & Co. Ltd
London · Glasgow · Sydney · Auckland
Toronto · Johannesburg

First published 1990
© Reginald Hill 1990

British Library Cataloguing in Publication Data

Hill, Reginald
  One small step.—(Crime Club)
  I. Title
  823′.914[F]

ISBN 0 00 232292 7

Photoset in Linotron Baskerville by
Rowland Phototypesetting Ltd
Bury St Edmunds, Suffolk
Printed in Great Britain by
William Collins Sons & Co. Ltd, Glasgow

To You

Dear Readers

without whom the writing would be in vain

and

To You

Still Dearer Purchasers

without whom the eating would be infrequent

THIS BOOK IS DEDICATED

in
appreciation
of
your loyalty

in
anticipation
of
your longevity

in
admiration
of
your taste

Non scribit, cuius carmina nemo legit

FOREWORD

We've been together now for twenty years. That's a lot of blood under the bridge. Sometimes 1970 seems like last weekend, sometimes it seems like ancient history. Famous men died—Forster who we thought already had, and de Gaulle who we imagined never would; Heath toppled Wilson, Solzhenitsyn won the Nobel Prize for Literature, Tony Jacklin won the US Open, and in September, Collins published *A Clubbable Woman*.

All right, so it wasn't the year's most earth-shaking event, but it meant a lot to me. And it must have meant a little to that hard core of loyal readers who kept on asking for more.

And of course to Andy Dalziel and Peter Pascoe, it meant the difference between life and death!

If time moves so erratically for me, how must it seem to that intermittently synchronous being, the series character? I mused on this the other day as I walked in the fells near my home. I'm not one of those writers who explain the creative process by saying, 'Then the characters take over.' On the page I'm a tyrant, but in my mind I let them run free, and as I walked I imagined I heard the dull thunder of Dalziel's voice, like a beer keg rolling down a cellar ramp.

'It's all right for him, poncing around up here, feeling all poetic about time and stuff. But what about us, eh? Just how old are we supposed to be anyway? I mean, if I were as old as it felt twenty years back when this lot started, how come I'm not getting meals-on-wheels and a free bus pass?'

'You're right,' answered Peter Pascoe's voice, higher, lighter, but just as querulous. 'Look at me. When *A Clubbable Woman* came out, I was a whizzkid sergeant, graduate entrant, potential high-flier. Twenty years on, I've just made chief inspector. That's not what I call whizzing, that's a long way from stratospheric!'

It was time to remind them what they were, figments of my imagination, paper and printers' ink not flesh and blood, and I started to formulate a few elegant phrases about the creative artist's use of a dual chronology.

'You mean,' interrupted Peter Pascoe, 'that we should regard historical time, i.e. your time, and fictive time, i.e. our time, as passenger trains running on parallel lines but at different speeds?'

'I couldn't have put it better myself,' I said. 'A perfect analogy to express the chronic dualism of serial literature.'

10

'Chronic's the bloody word,' growled Dalziel.

'Oh, do be quiet,' said Pascoe, with more courage than I ever gave him. 'Look, this is all very well, but analogies must be consistent. Parallel lines cannot converge in time, can they?'

'No, but they can pass through the same station, can't they?' I replied.

'You mean, as in *Under World*, where the references to the recent miners' strike clearly set the book in 1985?'

'Or 1986. I think I avoided that kind of specificity,' I said.

'You think so? Then what about *Bones and Silence* in which I return to work the February after I got injured in *Under World*, making it '87 at the latest, yet that book's full of specific dates, like Trinity Sunday falling on May 29th, which set it quite clearly in 1988?'

'You tell him, lad,' said Dalziel. 'Bugger thinks just because he's moved from Yorkshire into this sodding wilderness, he can get away scot-free with stunting our growth.'

'Think of your readers,' appealed Pascoe. 'Don't you have a duty to offer them some kind of explanation?'

'Bugger his readers!' roared Dalziel. 'What about us? Do you realize, if he dropped down dead now, which wouldn't surprise me, he'd leave you and me stuck where we are now, working forever? Is that fair, I ask you? Is that just?'

Lear-like, I was beginning to feel that handing over

control wasn't perhaps such a clever idea, but I knew how to deal with such imaginative insurrection. I headed home and poured myself a long Scotch, and then another. After a while I let out an appreciative burp, followed by a more genteel hiccup.

Now I could ponder in peace the implications of what I had heard.

There's no getting away from it—in twenty years, Dalziel and Pascoe have aged barely ten. But the readers for whom Pascoe expressed such concern don't seem to find it a problem. At least, none of them has mentioned it in their usually very welcome letters.

On the other hand a flattering and familiar coda to these letters on whatever topic is a pleasurable anticipation of further records of this ever-diverse pair. But if we are all ageing at twice their rate, there must come a time when . . .

But suddenly I jumped off this melancholy train of thought. Time can be speeded up as well as slowed down. I write, therefore they are! And what better birthday gift can I give my loyal readers than a quick trip into the future, nothing too conclusive, nothing to do with exit lines and bones and silence, but a reassuring glimpse of Pascoe when time has set a bit of a grizzle on his case, and of Dalziel still far from going gentle into that good night?

So here it is, my birthday gift. 'Bloody funny gift,' I hear Andy Dalziel mutter deep within. 'Have you clocked the price? And look at the length of it! There's more reading round a bag of chips.'

To which Peter Pascoe thoughtfully replies, 'Half-bottles cost more than fifty per cent of the full-bottle price because production costs stay constant. Besides, if this book deletes one tiny item from those endless lists of things unknown and deeds undone which trouble our sleeping and our dying, then it will be priceless.'

Dalziel's reply is unprintable. But, pricey or price-less, unless you've got the brass nerve to be reading this on a bookshop shelf, someone's paid for it. Accept my thanks. Next time, we'll be back to the present. Meanwhile, a very Happy Twentieth Birthday to us all!

Ravenglass
Cumbria

January 1990

ONE SMALL STEP

i

The first man to land on the moon was Neil Armstrong on July 20th, 1969. As he stepped off the module ladder, he said, 'One small step for a man, one giant leap for mankind.'

The first man to be murdered on the moon was Emile Lemarque on May 14th, 2010. As he fell off the module ladder, he said, '*Oh mer—*'

There were two hundred and twenty-seven million witnesses.

One of these was ex-Detective-Superintendent Andrew Dalziel who was only watching because the battery of his TV remote control had failed. What he really wanted to see was his favourite episode of *Star Trek* on the Nostalgia Channel. By comparison, Michelin-men bouncing dustily over lunar slag heaps made very dull viewing, particularly with the Yanks and Russkis leapfrogging each other to the edge of the solar system. But the Federated States of Europe had

15

waited a long time for their share of space glory and the Euro Channel had been ordered to give blanket coverage.

In the UK this met with a mixed response, and not just from those who preferred *Star Trek*. Britain's decision to opt out of the Federal Space Programme had always been controversial. During the years when it appeared the Programme's best hope of reaching the moon was via a ladder of wrecked rockets, the antis had smiled complacently and counted the money they were saving. But now the deed was done, the patriotic tabloids were demanding to know how come these inferior foreigners were prancing around in the Greatest Show Off Earth with no UK involvement whatever, unless you counted the use of English as the expedition's *lingua franca*? Even this was regarded by some as a slight, reducing the tongue of Shakespeare and Thatcher to a mere tool, like Esperanto.

But all most True Brits felt when they realized their choice of channels had been reduced from ninety-seven to ninety-six was a vague irritation which Andy Dalziel would probably have shared had he been able to switch over manually. Unfortunately he was confined to bed by an attack of gout, and irritation rapidly boiled into rage, especially as his visiting nurse, who had retired to the kitchen for a recuperative smoke, ignored all his cries for help. It took a violent splintering explosion to bring her running, white-faced, into the bedroom.

Dalziel was sinking back into his pillows, flushed

with the effort and the triumph of having hurled his useless remote control through the telly screen.

'Now look what you've made me do,' he said. 'Don't just stand there. Fetch me another set. I'm missing *Star Trek*.'

It took three days for it to emerge that what the two hundred and twenty-seven million witnesses had seen wasn't just an unhappy accident but murder.

Till then, most of the UK press coverage had been concerned with interpreting the dead man's possibly unfinished last words. The favourite theory was that *Oh mer . . .* was simply *oh mère*, a dying man's appeal to his mother, though the Catholic *Lozenge* stretched this piously to *Oh mère de Dieu*. When it was suggested that a life member of the *Société Athéiste et Humaniste de France* (Lourdes branch) would be unlikely to trouble the Virgin with his dying breath, the *Lozenge* tartly retorted that history was crammed with deathbed conversions. The *Jupiter*, whose aged owner ascribed his continued survival to just such a conversion during his last heart attack, showed its sympathy for this argument by adopting Camden's couplet in its leader headline—BETWIXT THE MODULE AND THE GROUND, MERCY HE ASKED, MERCY HE FOUND. The *Defender*, taking this literally, suggested that if indeed Lemarque had been going to say *Oh merci*, this was less likely to be a plea for divine grace than an expression of ironic gratitude, as in, 'Well, thanks a bunch for bringing me so far, then chopping me off at the knees!' The *Planet* meanwhile had torpedoed the *oh mère* theory to its own satisfaction by the discovery that Lemarque's mother was an Algerian migrant worker who had sold her unwanted child to a baby farm with many evil results, not the least of which was the *Planet*'s headline—WOG DOG FLOGGED FROG SPROG. Ultimately the child had come into the hands of a Lourdes couple who treated him badly and *never took him to the seaside* (the *Planet*'s italics), persuading the editor that this poor deprived foreigner had reverted to infancy in the face of annihilation and was once again pleading to be taken *au mer*. Chortling with glee, the *Intransigent* pointed out that *mer* was feminine and congratulated the *Planet* on now being illiterate in two languages. Then it rather surrendered its superior position by speculating that, coming from Lourdes, Lemarque might have fantasized that he was falling into the famous healing pool and started to cry, *Eau merveilleux!*

It took the staid *Autograph* to say what all the French papers had agreed from the start—that Lemarque was merely exclaiming, like any civilized Gaul in a moment of stress, *Oh merde!*

But it was the *Spheroid* who scooped them all by revealing under the banner CASE OF THE EXPIRING FROG! that the Eurofed Department of Justice was treating Lemarque's death as murder.

Even Dalziel's attention was engaged by this news. For weeks the Current Affairs Channel had been stagnant with speculation about the new German Question. Two things had happened since the euphoria of the early 'nineties when a reunified Germany had agreed to a continued, though diminishing, Soviet presence in the East and US presence in the West. First, the hardliners had regained control in Moscow and *glasnost* was dead. Secondly, the new Germany had become increasingly irritated with its military guests and increasingly fretful over certain of its frontiers. So now, in the kind of simplification so beloved of the media, the stark choice facing the Great Powers was either to withdraw and let Europe resolve its own destiny, or to advance and confront each other once again along the old pre-1990 boundary.

All this Dalziel found rather less enthralling than non-alcoholic lager. But a murder on the moon had a touch of originality which set his nerve ends tingling, particularly when it emerged that the man most likely to be in charge of the case was the UK Commissioner in the Eurofed Justice Department, none other than his old friend and former colleague, Peter Pascoe.

'I taught that lad everything he knows,' he boasted as he watched Pascoe's televised press conference from Strasbourg.

'Lad?' snorted Miss Montague, his new nurse, who could snatch and press her own considerable weight and whose rippling muscles filled Dalziel with nostalgic lust. 'He looks almost as decrepit as you!'

Dalziel grunted a promise of revenge as extreme,

and as impotent, as Lear's, and turned up the sound on his new set.

Pascoe was saying, 'In effect, what was at first thought to be a simple though tragic systems failure resulting in a short circuit in the residual products unit of his TEC, that is Total Environment Costume, sometimes called lunar suit, appears after more detailed examination by American scientists working in the US lunar village, for the use of whose facilities may I take this chance to say we are truly thankful, to have been deliberately induced.'

For a moment all the reporters were united in deep incomprehension. The man from the *Onlooker* raised his eyebrows and the woman from the *Defender* lowered her glasses; some scribbled earnestly as if they understood everything, others yawned ostentatiously as if there were nothing to understand. Dalziel chortled and said, 'The bugger doesn't get any better.' But it took the man from the *Spheroid* to put the necessary probing question—'You wha'?'

Patiently Pascoe resumed. 'Not to put too fine a point on it, and using layman's language, the microcircuitry of the residual products unit of his TEC had been deliberately cross-linked with both the main and the reserve power systems in such a manner that it needed only the addition of a conductive element, in this case liquescent, to complete the circuit with unfortunate, that is, fatal, consequences.'

Now the reporters were united in a wild surmise.

The *Onlooking* eyebrows were lowered, the *Defending* spectacles raised. But once again it was the earnest seeker of enlightenment from the *Spheroid* who so well expressed what everyone was thinking. 'You mean he pissed himself to death?'

Dalziel laughed so much he almost fell out of bed, though the nurse noted with interest that some internal gyroscope kept his brimming glass of Lucozade steady in his hand. Recovering, he downed the drink in a single gulp and, still chuckling, listened once more to his erstwhile underling.

Pascoe was explaining, 'While there would certainly be a severe shock, this was not of itself sufficient to be fatal. But the short circuit was induced in such a way as to drain completely and immediately all power from the TEC, cutting dead all systems, including the respiratory unit. It was the shock that made him fall. But it was the lack of oxygen that killed him, before the dust had started to settle.'

This sobered the gathering a little. But newsmen's heartstrings vibrate less plangently than their dead-lines and soon Pascoe was being bombarded with questions about the investigation, which he fielded so blandly and adroitly that finally Dalziel switched off in disgust.

'What's up?' asked Miss Montague. 'I thought you taught him everything he knows.'

'So I did,' said Dalziel. 'But one thing I could never teach the bugger was how to tell reporters to sod off!'

21

He poured himself another glass of Lucozade. The nurse seized the bottle and raised it to her nostrils.

'I think this has gone off,' she said.

'Tastes all right to me,' said Dalziel. 'Try a nip.'

Miss Montague poured herself a glass, raised it, sipped it delicately.

'You know,' she said thoughtfully, 'you could be right.'

'I usually am,' said Dalziel. 'Cheers!'

At nine that night the telephone rang.

'This is a recording,' said Dalziel. 'If you want to leave a message, stick it in a bottle.'

'You sound very jolly,' said Pascoe.

'Well, I've supped a lot of Lucozade,' said Dalziel, looking at the gently snoring figure of Nurse Montague on the sofa opposite. 'What's up?'

'Just a social call. Did you see me on the box?'

'I've got better things to do than listen to civil bloody servants being civil and servile,' growled Dalziel.

'Oh, you did see it, then. That's what we call diplomatic language out here in the real world,' said Pascoe.

'Oh aye. Up here it's called soft soap and it's very good for enemas.'

Pascoe laughed and said, 'All right, Andy. I never could fool you, could I? Yes, this whole thing has got a great crap potential. To start with, we reckon the Yanks deliberately leaked their suspicion of foul play to bounce us into letting them take full control of the investigation. Now, we're not terribly keen on that idea.'

'Oh aye? Don't they have jurisdiction anyway?'

'Certainly not. Space is international by UN treaty. But they're established up there with all the facilities, so on the surface it's a generous, neighbourly offer, only . . . Look, it's a bit complicated . . .'

'Come on, lad, I'm not quite gaga and I do read the papers still,' snarled Dalziel. 'It's this German business, isn't it? Lots of people, especially the Yanks, think it'd be daft to remove all control from the Krauts. Some 'cos they reckon after *ein Volk* and *ein Reich*, it's not a big step to *ein Führer*. Some 'cos they reckon that hotting up the Cold War's the best way of getting them big defence dollars rolling again. And some 'cos they've believed all along that all that 1990 did was put a big red rump on NATO!'

'I don't quite see—' began Pascoe.

'Don't go all diplomatic on me, lad. You've not got the eyebrows for it. I'll spell it out, shall I? The Yanks' preferred option is more troops and bases in Germany even if it means seeing the brickies back on the Wall again. But they know they can't manage this without Eurofed backing. Their best bet for support there is France—typical of the Frogs, no one knows which way they're going to jump. But one thing's for sure, it'll be emotion not logic that sets them hopping.

'Us Brits on the other hand are famous for our rationality, and because the Yanks have banned all

British supporters from the World Cup Finals in Florida, we'll bust a gut to get them buggers chucked out of Germany!

'But the Frogs hold the key. Which means, anything that gets them and the Krauts at each other's goolies just now will look like very good news to the Yanks and lousy news to us.

'Conclusion. The Americans have elected the German crew member number one suspect, and you reckon any investigation they mount will make bloody sure that's where the finger points. How's that for a bit of close political analysis?'

'Marvellous,' breathed Pascoe admiringly. 'Who speaks so well should never speak in vain.'

'I don't know about in vain, but I do prefer in plain English. So what have they got on this German, then?'

There was a long pause.

'Come on, lad,' said Dalziel. 'They must have a pretty good case against him, else you'd not be so worried.'

'Yes, they do. But it's not . . . Look, Andy. I'm sorry, but the thing is, security. You're not cleared for this. It's a need-to-know classification and the only people who need to know outside of government are the investigating officers. So I really can't tell you any more. Not unless I appointed you an investigating officer!'

He said this with a light dismissive laugh, but Dalziel

had had many years' experience of interpreting Pascoe's light laughs.

'All right, lad,' he said softly. 'What's going off? Spit it out and make it quick, else this phone goes back down so hard it'll need a jemmy to prise it back up.'

'There's no fooling you, is there, Andy?' said Pascoe. 'OK. Straight it is. I've been asked to take charge of the case, not because I'm the best, but because I'm not French, German, Spanish, Italian, Dutch, Danish or Irish. Meaning none of the countries actually involved in the *Europa*'s mission will trust any of the others to give them a fair deal! They've given me a free hand. They've also given me four days to get a result.'

'*Any* result?'

'The truth, Andy,' said Pascoe heavily. 'That's the result I'm looking for.'

'Only asking,' said Dalziel. 'So how come you're wasting time talking to a clapped-out candidate for the boneyard?'

'Andy, I need eyes and I need a nose. All right, I know I could have any of the Yard's top men for the asking. Only, nowadays they get to the top by being on top of the technology and that's no use to me here. Technology's a two-way ticket. If you live by it, you can be fooled by it. Also the Yard's best will still be on the way up. Europe's wide open to an ambitious man nowadays. But ambitious men need to tread carefully, else when their names come up for advancement there can be more vetoes in the air than flies round a dustbin. So what I need is a seat-of-the-pants copper with a bloodhound's nose, who's got nothing to lose or to gain, and who doesn't give a tuppenny toss about any bugger. I fed this data into my computer and it let out a huge burp. So I picked up the phone and I rang you, Andy. What do you say?'

'You cheeky sod!' exclaimed Dalziel. 'I say you must be off your trolley! My nose is so out of practice I can hardly tell Orkney from Islay. As for seat-of-the-pants, I've been stuck in bed with gout for nigh on a fortnight, and I don't want no jokes either.'

'Who's laughing? Andy, what you clearly need is a place where you won't have to worry about putting pressure on your foot, and I can help you there.'

'Hold on,' said Dalziel. 'I didn't quite get that. This must be a bad line. You *are* talking about bringing the *Europa*'s crew back to Earth for investigation, aren't you? Well, *aren't you?*'

'Andy!' said Pascoe reprovingly. 'First thing you taught me was, good investigation starts at the scene of the crime. And anyway, you always expected the moon from me. So how can you turn me down now that I'm finally offering it to you?'

ii

Space travel weren't so bad after all, thought Andy Dalziel. It put him in mind of an occasion half a century ago when he'd supped about twenty pints and ended up on his back in a rowing boat drifting slowly down the cut, looking up at a midnight sky, heavy and dark as a nautch-girl's tits, all studded with a thousand stars.

He should have realized how easy it must be when Pascoe told him the Yanks had dumped a minority party senator and his wife to make room for them on their state-of-the-art lunar shuttle which had been ferrying distinguished visitors to the moon for half a decade. But he'd still been protesting even as Pascoe urged him into the soft yielding couch.

'What's going off?' he demanded in alarm. 'This thing's trying to feel me up!'

'It's all right,' assured Pascoe. 'It's just a wrap-around fabric to hold you in place when we achieve weightlessness. Honestly, it'll just be like riding in a limo, without any traffic jams.'

'If it's so bloody easy, why's the Federation making such a big thing about it?'

'It's like going up Mont Blanc,' explained Pascoe patiently. 'You can either book a table at the summit restaurant and take the scenic railway or you can pack your sarnies into your rucksack and climb. That way

27

it's harder, but you get a lot more Brownie points. More important in the long run, it establishes the Federation's right to be there. Space is international now, but there may come a time when the carving up starts, and we don't want to be scavenging for crumbs under the Americans' chair.'

'Bloody hell,' said Dalziel. 'I'll leave the politicking to you, lad. I'll stick to nicking villains. If I survive the trip, that is.'

In fact, he was feeling better than he'd done for some time. The doctor had confirmed that his heart was in good order for a man of his age. He'd been more concerned about the high blood pressure related to Dalziel's gout, but the drugs Dalziel was taking seemed to have this under control, and reluctantly he'd given the go-ahead. Now as the shuttle came swooping in over the moon's surface, the fat man was delighted to find that his gout symptoms had almost completely vanished.

'You were right, lad,' he admitted. 'There's nowt to this astronaut business.'

'Not this way,' agreed Pascoe. 'Mind you, *Europa*'s not so luxurious.'

'Can't be, if they're still crapping in their breeks,' said Dalziel.

'Andy, I thought I'd explained,' said Pascoe long-sufferingly. 'They only need their TECs for moving around the moon's surface. In the mother ship they just wear light tunics. The TECs were kept in the hold.

Each crew member has his or her own locker and each suit is individually tailored and has a name tag stuck to it, so it's quite clear that whoever tampered with Lemarque's was aiming at him and no one else. Now, have you got it?'

'All right, I'm with you,' said Dalziel. 'No need to go on about things. Christ, have you looked down there? It's like the M1 on a Bank Holiday. All dug up and no bugger working? Where's this village at?'

'Let's see. Yes, there it is, down there, in the Sea of Tranquillity.'

'Those pimples? Looks like an outbreak of chicken pox.'

Dalziel wasn't altogether wrong. The Village, a complex of sealed domes linked by corridors, covering about five acres, did indeed resemble a patch of blisters on the lunar skin till their third braking orbit brought out the scale of the thing. Next time round, one of the domes loomed large before them, threatening collision, and then they were slipping smoothly into a docking bay, and suddenly the stars were out of sight.

The Commander of the Lunar Village was waiting to greet them. He was a small balding astrophysicist with a nervous manner who reminded Dalziel of a snout who'd been foolish enough to feed him duff information twenty years earlier. With good behaviour the man should be getting out shortly.

The Commander passed them over with speed and

unconcealable relief to his Head of Security, Colonel Ed Druson, who was a lean and wiry black man with the stretched look of an athlete who has carried his twenties training schedules into his forties.

'Welcome to the moon,' he said, offering his hand. 'Hope you had a good trip.'

'Aye, it were grand,' said Dalziel, bouncing gently up and down to test the effect of low gravity on his gouty foot. Delighted to feel no pain, he went on, 'Only thing is, that space ship of thine didn't seem to have a bar, and it's thirsty work travelling.'

'Andy,' said Pascoe warningly. 'Should you, with your gout?'

'Bugger the gout,' said Dalziel. 'I've got a throat like a spinster's tit. I could even thole bourbon if you've not got the real stuff.'

'I'll see what we can do,' said Druson, clearly wondering what the hell the Brits were up to, filling valuable shuttle space with an overweight, geriatric alcoholic who had gout.

He went on, 'Like we told your people, *Europa*'s in a parking orbit with one of our guys acting nightwatch. We've got the crew in our new accommodation dome. We're expanding our technical staff and they don't start arriving till the weekend.'

'We should be finished well before then,' said Pascoe confidently.

'Yeah? Well, you sure ought to be,' said Druson. 'Looks like an open and shut case. Could have saved yourselves the bother of a trip, I reckon. You've seen our file on the German? Jesus, you Euros surely know how to pick 'em!'

To Dalziel it sounded like a just rebuke. Pascoe had provided him with copies of all the astronauts' files plus the American incident report. This contained statements from the *Europa* crew, setting out where they were and what they were doing at the time of the fatality, plus Druson's own analysis and conclusions. He saw little reason to look further than Kaufmann as culprit, and offered two pieces of concrete evidence and a motive.

The first pointer was an entry in Lemarque's private journal, removed from his locker in a search of doubtful legality. Several of the astronauts kept such journals with an eye to a literary future after their flying days were over. Lermarque's consisted mainly of fluorescently purple prose about the beauties of space with mention of his colleagues kept down to a dismissive minimum. Then at the end of a much polished speech in which he told the world of his sense of honour at being the first Euro, and more importantly, the first Frenchman, to step out on to the moon's surface, he had scribbled almost indecipherably, *Ka s'en fâche. Gardes-toi!*

Ka is getting angry. Watch out!

Was *Ka* Kaufmann? Druson had asked. And the discovery during the same illegal search of a micro-probe in the German's locker had deepened his suspicions. A gloss for the non-technical pointed out that a microprobe was a kind of electronic screwdriver which would have been necessary in the readjustment of the TEC circuits.

But there was still the question of motive. And why was Ka getting angry?

'Blackmail,' Druson replied promptly. 'You've read the file. It's obvious.'

It certainly appeared so. The major part of the American report was a digest of a CIA investigation which concluded that Captain Dieter Kaufmann had been passing military secrets to Moscow ever since he joined the German airforce four years after his arrival from Leipzig during the great trek west of 1989.

'You're saying he was a KGB plant at fourteen?' said Pascoe sceptically.

'They're big on long-term planning,' said Druson. 'Read the evidence.'

It was detailed and unanswerable. And it hadn't been compiled overnight.

'It would have been neighbourly to pass this information on a little earlier,' suggested Pascoe mildly. 'Say three years earlier.'

It was three years since Kaufmann had joined the *Europa* crew.

'We like to be sure of our facts in such a serious matter,' said Druson.

Also, thought Pascoe, Kaufmann's full-time transfer into the Eurospace programme had removed him from access to NATO information and left him with nothing to pass on but astro-technology which in Russian and American terms was yesterday's news. With no threat to themselves, the Americans had decided to keep their information under their hat till they could make maximum profit from it.

Now that moment had come.

'Can we look at the body?' said Pascoe. 'Just for the record.'

'Sure. But it ain't very pretty.'

Dalziel had seen a lot worse.

'Not very big, is he?' said Pascoe.

'Depends where you're looking,' said Dalziel.

He turned away from the body and picked up the Frenchman's TEC which was also on display.

'I bet he fancied himself too,' he said. 'These little fellows often do.'

'Why do you say that, Andy?' asked Pascoe.

'His name tag for a start.'

Instead of following a horizontal line, the adhesive name strip had been adjusted to a jaunty thirty degrees angle echoing the shoulder seam.

'Used to get buggers in the Force who tried to tart up their uniforms like that,' said Dalziel, sniffing at the headpiece. 'And they usually wore aftershave that'd kill mosquitoes too.'

'Seems he did have a reputation for being a cocky little bastard,' said Druson, looking at Dalziel with a new respect.

Pascoe said, 'And the circuitry was definitely interfered with?'

'Oh yeah. Clear as a fox among chickens. Rush job by the look of it. Well, it would have to be, in the *Europa*'s hold. No time for finesse.'

'No,' agreed Pascoe. 'Seen enough, Andy?'

'More than enough. I'd got to thinking the next dead 'un I saw would be me.'

'Good Lord,' said Pascoe. 'When did you start believing in an afterlife?'

'Man who lets himself be talked into flying to the moon to stare at a dead Frog's got no right to disbelieve *anything*,' said Dalziel. 'Did someone say something about a room with a bed in it?'

'Let's go,' said Druson.

He led them to their quarters, two small bedrooms with a shared living-room. When the door had shut behind him, Dalziel said, 'OK, lad. What do you reckon? Still a fit-up by the Yanks?'

'Open mind,' said Pascoe. 'They've certainly put a reasonable case together. Maybe Kaufmann did do it.'

'Mebbe. I'd trust 'em a lot more if yon black bugger hadn't managed to forget that Glenmorangie he promised me!'

Pascoe grinned and said, 'A good night's sleep will do you more good, Andy. Nothing more to be done till the morning or whatever they call it up here. Then it'll be straight down to the interrogations.'

'Hold on,' said Dalziel. 'Scene of the crime, remember? That's why you said we had to come here, and you were dead right. Only this isn't the scene, is it? The Frog dropped dead somewhere out there. And the actual scene of the real crime is floating around somewhere up there. Shouldn't we fix up to visit the *Europa* before we do owt else?'

'Don't worry,' said Pascoe. 'I'll be arranging a trip as soon as possible. But time's too short to waste, so in the morning let's get on with talking to the crew, shall we? Now I thought we'd work individually. I'll take three and you take three, then we'll swap over like a sort of reverse singles . . .'

'It's not bloody tennis!' said Dalziel obstinately. 'I'll need to ask what these sods got up to on *Europa* and unless I've seen *Europa*, what they say won't make bloody sense, will it?'

There was a tap at the door. Pascoe didn't move. Dalziel scowled at him and went to answer it.

A smiling young man handed him two litre-sized bottles saying, 'There you go, pops.'

'Pops!' said Pascoe as Dalziel closed the door. 'You must be mellowing, Andy. Time was when you'd have nutted anyone who spoke to you like that.'

'That was when I was young and daft,' said Dalziel, removing the seal from one of the bottles. 'At my age, anyone who gives me two litres of Glenmorangie can call me Mavis if he likes. You want a splash?'

'Only water,' said Pascoe. 'I'll have a shower. Then

I'll work out a schedule for the interrogations before I go to bed. OK?'

He spoke defiantly. Dalziel stared at him for a moment, then shrugged.

'Fine,' he said. 'You're the boss now.'

'So I am,' smiled Pascoe as he left. 'So I am.'

'And I'm to be Queen of the May, Mother,' murmured Dalziel raising the bottle to his lips. 'I'm to be Queen of the May!'

iii

Dalziel had a bad night. He dreamt he challenged Nurse Montague to the best of three falls and lost by a straight submission. It wouldn't have been so bad if the dream had been erotic but it was merely humiliating and he woke up dry and droopy as a camel's tail. Whisky only washed his black thoughts blacker and when finally there came a tap on the door and Pascoe's voice invited him to go to breakfast, he snarled, 'Sod off!' He was still not washed or dressed half an hour later when Pascoe returned with a cup of coffee and a chocolate doughnut, and, even worse, the kind of sympathetic smile usually reserved for tedious old relatives in twilight homes.

Only the younger man's offer to call the Village

medics and have someone check him out got Dalziel
out of bed. He was still running his portable electric
razor over the shadowy planet of his face as they made
their way to the *Europa* crew's dome, and this at last
provoked an honestly irritated response from Pascoe.

'For heaven's sake, Andy, put that thing away. We
are representing the Federal Justice Department, after
all!'

With his first twinge of pleasure of the day, Dalziel
slipped the slim plastic razor case into his breast pocket
and followed Pascoe into the dome.

The six survivors of the *Europa* crew were an interesting
assortment. It was almost possible to identify them by
racial characteristics alone.

The two women were easiest. The Dane, Marte
Schierbeck, was pure Viking, long-bodied, long-faced,
and grey-eyed, with hair so fair it was almost silver.
By contrast the Spaniard, Silvia Rabal, was compact
and curvaceous, with huge dark eyes, full pouting lips,
and a rather prominent, slightly hooked nose. Her jet
black hair was razored back above her ears and
sculpted into a rose-tipped crest. The total effect was
arrestingly beautiful, like some colourful exotic bird.

Of the men, a rather spidery figure with a face
crumpled like an old banknote and eyes blue as the
lakes of Killarney had to be the Irishman, Kevin
O'Meara, while a Rembrandt burgher, solid of frame
and stolid of feature, was typecast as the Dutchman,

Adriaan van der Heyde. Only the German and the Italian ran counter to type with the six-foot, blue-eyed blond turning out to be Marco Albertosi, which meant the black-haired, volatile-faced, lean-figured gondolier was Dieter Kaufmann.

Pascoe introduced himself formally, explaining Dalziel simply as his assistant. He made heavy weather of insisting on the serious nature of the affair and the absoluteness of his own authority, and by the time he finished by saying, 'The investigation will be carried on in English since, perhaps regrettably, neither Mr Dalziel nor myself are fluent in any of your languages,' he had succeeded in relaxing the crew into a union of mocking anglophobia, which was precisely what he intended. In his own case the linguistic disclaimer was a downright lie. He was fluent in French, German and Italian, and could get by in the rest. In Dalziel's case . . . well, he'd learned a long time ago that it was dangerous to assume his ignorance about *anything*!

'We will start with individual interviews,' said Pascoe. 'Herr Kaufmann, would you come with me? Mr Dalziel . . .'

Pascoe had already decreed the order of interview, but Dalziel let his eyes slowly traverse the group with the speculative gaze of a sailor in a brothel. Then, with a macho aggression which should have sat ill on a man of his age, but didn't, he stabbed a huge forefinger at Silvia Rabal and said, 'I'll have *her*!'

Space was short for special interview facilities so the

38

interrogations took place in the newcomers' rooms. Rabal sat on the bed without being asked. Dalziel eased himself carefully on to a frail-looking chair and began to open the second bottle of malt.

'Drink?' he said.

'No. Why have you picked me first?' she asked in a rather harsh voice.

'Well, I said to myself, if she's the one who killed the Frog, mebbe she'll try to seduce me to keep me quiet.'

The woman's huge eyes opened even wider as she ran this through her mental translator to make sure she'd got it right. Then she drew back her head and laughed, no avian screech but a full-throated Carmen laugh, sensual, husky, sending tremors down her body like the inviting ripples on a jungle pool.

'Perhaps I will have that drink, Dalziel,' she said.

'Thought you might,' he said, handing her a glass.

She held it close to her breast so he had to lean over her to pour. She looked up at him and breathed, 'Enough.' Her breath was honeyed, or more precisely spiced as if she had been eating cinammon and coriander. Such perfumes from a restaurant kitchen would have alarmed Dalziel, who liked his food plain dressed, but from the warm oven of this woman's mouth, they were disturbingly appetitive, setting juices running he thought had long since dried to a trickle.

He sat down heavily and the frail chair spread its legs, but held.

'Cheers,' she said, lifting her glass to her lips.

'Cheers,' he answered. It was time to grasp the initiative.

'Look, love,' he said. 'Cards on the table, that's the way I work. That Pascoe, now, he's different, a right sly bugger, you'll need to keep an eye on him. Me, though, I'm not clever enough to be cunning. But God gave me a fair share of good Yorkshire common sense, and that tells me you're about the least likely suspect of the lot, and *that's* the real reason I picked you first. So I can get some answers I can be sure are honest.'

She said, 'Thank you. I am flattered. But how do you work this out?'

'For a start, you weren't on the module, were you? You stayed on *Europa* to look after the shop, you and the Eyetie. So while the module party all had plenty of reason to be mucking about with their TECs in the hold, you didn't.'

'And this is when this interference was done, you think?'

'Has to be, hasn't it?'

'I suppose. This fault in Emile's suit, could it not be just a fault? That American tells us nothing, just makes hints.'

'No. It were deliberate interference, no doubt,' said Dalziel with the technological certainty of a man who used to repair police radios with his truncheon. 'Must've been done in a hurry. I mean, given time, I expect you lot are all clued up enough to have covered your tracks.'

'Oh yes, I think so.' She regarded him thoughtfully. 'So I am in the clear because I stay on the ship? Then Marco who stayed with me must be clear too?'

'That depends if his legs are as pretty as yours,' leered Dalziel. 'But why do you ask? Would it surprise you if Marco was innocent?'

'No. I do not say that.'

'But he didn't get on with Lemarque, is that it?'

'They were not good friends, no. But not so bad that he would kill!'

'How bad does that have to be for an Italian?' wondered Dalziel. 'Why'd they not like each other? Rivals, were they? Or maybe that had a lovers' tiff?'

'I'm sorry?'

'You know. If they had something going between 'em, and they fell out . . .'

He made a limp-wristed rocking gesture.

'What do you say?' she cried indignantly. 'That is not possible!'

'No? Well, there's things in these files as'd amaze you,' he said, patting the pile of folders on the floor next to him. 'Do you not have fairy tales in Spain, then? Kiss a frog and you get yourself a princess, that sort of thing?'

Puzzlement, irritation, and something else besides were chasing each other across that expressive face.

'You are mistaken, I think,' she said, recovering her

41

poise. 'They were rivals, yes. Each wanting to be the most macho, that is all.'

'You reckon? Mebbe they didn't bother you much. I'll be interested to hear what that Danish lass made of them. She's a lot more boyish than you, might have turned them on a bit more . . .'

She looked ready to explode, recovered again and said, 'Yes, if you are interested in low-temperature physics, go to her.'

'No, thanks. Me, I prefer the high-temperature Latin type,' he said lecherously.

She gave him a thin smile and said, 'You talk a lot, Dalziel. Can you, I wonder—what is the phrase?—put your money where your mouth is?'

'Depends where you want me to put my mouth,' said Dalziel negligently. 'Thanks for the offer, but. Mebbe later when I've a minute to spare, eh?' Or a week, he thought ruefully. Though there had been a time . . . At least his diversionary tactics had worked.

'Offer? What offer? You do not think . . .' Suddenly she broke into indignant Spanish.

Dalziel yawned and said, 'Stick to English, luv. If a man's worth swearing at, he's worth swearing at in his own language. Now, I've read all the statements but I'm not much good at technical stuff, so mebbe you can give us a hand. First, these TECs, once they were activated in the module, you could monitor their circuits on *Europa*, is that right?'

'Yes.'

'And from *Europa* this info would go back to Earth Control?'

'Yes. There is non-stop transmission of pictures and technical data from *Europa* to Earth.'

'Aye,' scowled Dalziel. 'Made me miss *Star Trek*. But weren't there a transmission blackout from *Europa* as the module went down?'

'That is right. There was an electrical storm.'

He whistled and said, 'That must have been scary.'

'No,' she said with professional indifference. 'It happens often. Fortunately it did not last long and we got pictures back in time for the big event. Emile stepping on to the moon, I mean, not . . .'

She shuddered. A sympathetic smile lit Dalziel's face like a wrecker's lantern and he said, 'Don't take on, lass. Now, let's see. It were just *Europa*'s Earth transmissions that were affected? You still kept your contact with the module?'

'There was a little interference but we still got pictures.'

'And technical data on the TEC circuits?'

'Yes,' she snapped with the growing exasperation of the expert at being made to repeat the obvious. Dalziel scratched his nose. To him, such exasperation was the reddening skin above a boxer's eye. You pounded at it till it split.

'And there was no sign of owt wrong with Lemarque's suit? No hint that his circuits had been mucked around?'

43

'I have said so in my statement!' she cried. 'There was nothing till the moment when he made water. Then pouf! it is finished. No one can say it was my fault! There were two of us watching. It was a systems malfunction I think, no one to blame. Who has been blaming me. . .?"

'Calm down, woman!' bellowed Dalziel. 'You'll be gabbling away in Spanish again just now, and then where will we be? Have another drink. That's it, straight down. If you buggers drank more of this stuff and less of that gangria, you'd mebbe not need to run around screaming like banshees and slaughtering bulls. Now, get it into your noddle, nobody's blaming you, least of all me. So, just a couple more questions . . .'

iv

Pascoe and Dalziel had agreed to confer between interviews.

'Anything?' asked Pascoe.

'She's been bonking either the Italian or the Frog or mebbe both, and she doesn't much care for the Dane, so mebbe she got in on the act too. And she says that Albertosi and Lemarque didn't much hit it off.'

'She volunteered all this?'

'I prodded a bit. Told her I suspected they were a couple of poofters.'

'Oh Andy. Any more disinformation I should know about?'

'I told her you were a right bastard, and I said she weren't on my list of suspects.'

'And isn't she?'

'You know me, lad. *You*'re on my list till I get the evidence to cross you off. She certainly had less chance than the others of fiddling with Lemarque's suit. Mind you, she got very agitated when she thought I was hinting she were to blame for not monitoring the TEC transmissions properly. That electrical storm checked out, did it?'

'Happens all the time, evidently. And there were two of them doing the monitoring.'

'Aye. I take it, from what you're saying, you haven't clamped the Kraut in irons? Not even for spying? He is a spy, I take it?'

'Oh yes, no question. He doesn't deny it.'

Dalziel considered, then said gently, 'Now that should be a great big plus for the Yanks' theory that he knocked the Frog off. So why do I get the feeling it's nowt of the sort?'

Pascoe regarded him blankly. Time was when Dalziel reckoned he could have followed most of his old colleague's thought-processes along a broad spoor of telltale signs, but not any more. Perhaps time had dulled his perception. Or perhaps it had honed Pascoe's control.

Then the younger man smiled and was his old self again.

'I'm glad to see the nose is getting back into shape, Andy,' he said. 'The truth is, I knew all about Kaufmann's relations with the East long before Druson told me. As usual, the CIA have only managed to get half a story. The more important half is that Kaufmann's a double, always has been. Oddly enough, that's partly the reason he got into the Fed's space programme in the first place. He's a high flier in every sense and was due a promotion. The East were licking their lips as the logical career step would have taken him into a very sensitive area of missile guidance. His own people recognized how hard it would be to keep up his act with duff info at this level, so someone came up with the bright idea of nominating him for the moon shot. That way, he kept his cred with the East by passing them what is in their terms a lot of relatively antiquated space technology. The Yanks were right about that at least!'

He laughed, inviting Dalziel to join in his amusement. But the fat man was not to be manipulated so easily.

'Fuck me rigid!' he said angrily. 'Why the hell didn't you tell me this before?'

'*Need-to-know*, remember, Andy? Look, for all I knew, the Americans had got it right, Kaufmann was the killer, and I was into damage-limitation. I didn't see a need to load you down with classified stuff that wasn't necessary.'

Dalziel swallowed his irritation with difficulty and said, 'Meaning, now you've talked, he's definitely off your list?'

'Ninety per cent, I'd say. But I'd still like your opinion, Andy, and it'll be a better opinion now you know this spy business didn't really figure as motive.'

'Because if Lemarque *had* threatened to tell the Fed that Kaufmann was an agent, it wouldn't be much of a threat, as they know already?'

'Right.'

'But suppose he was threatening to tell the East that Kaufmann was a double?'

'In that case,' said Pascoe quietly, 'Kaufmann would have told us and Lemarque would have been taken care of much more discreetly.'

Dalziel digested this, then shook his head unhappily and said, 'Oh, Pete, Pete. Listen, lad, I'm far too old a dog to be learning new tricks. If this is a good old-fashioned killing because some bugger's been dipping his hand or his wick where he shouldn't, that's fine. But if it's spies and politics and that kind of crap, better beam me down to the twilight zone.'

Pascoe smiled and said in a kindly tone, 'I think you're mixing your programmes, Andy. And if you're going to try for pathos, better lose a bit of weight. Look, why do you think I brought you along? I've learnt enough new tricks to deal with the politics, but some of the old tricks may have gone a bit rusy. If it *is* just a good old-fashioned killing, and it could be, I'm relying on you to sort it out. You're my fail-safe, Andy. OK? Now let's get on. I've got the Irishman and you've got the Dane. And try to hold back on the Hamlet jokes, won't you?'

Marte Schierbeck was a very different proposition from Silvia Rabal. The atmosphere had changed from Mediterranean heat to Nordic coldness, but a native Yorkshireman knows better than to trust in mere weather. A fragment of hymn from his distant Sunday School days drifted through Dalziel's mind as he met the woman's cool grey eyes.

> A man who looks on glass
> On it may stay his eye,
> Or if he pleases through it pass . . .

He said, 'Was Emile more jealous of Marco than the other way round, do you think?'

She expressed no surprise but simply asked, 'What has Silvia said?'

'Does it matter?'

'The truth matters. We must tell the truth, mustn't we? Especially to policemen.' She spoke with no apparent irony.

48

'That's how it works in Denmark, is it? Do you do lecture tours?'

'Sorry?'

'Just my little joke. So what about Marco, then? Was he very jealous of Emile?'

'All men are jealous of their successors. That is why they hate their sons.'

'Jesus,' said Dalziel.

'There too,' said the woman.

A man who looks on glass . . . Dalziel made a determined effort to refocus.

'Was it you who broke off the affair, then?' he asked.

'*Affair*,' she echoed.

Not even his gout had made Dalziel feel older than the delicate way in which she savoured the old-worldliness of the word.

'Yes,' she went on. 'I broke it off. That is perhaps why Marco was jealous, not because he cared about having me, but because I let him see I did not care about having him. But I think what you are really asking is, "Was he jealous enough to kill?" Perhaps. He is Italian, and their self-image permits crimes of passion.'

'Not much passion in fixing a man's space suit so that first time he passes water he drops down dead,' sneered Dalziel, suddenly keen to pierce this icy carapace.

It was like spitting on a glacier.

She said, 'To the Latin mind, it might seem . . . apt.'

Dalziel didn't reply at once and the woman, mistaking his silence, tried to help him over his repression.

'Because the electrical connection which killed him would be through his sex organ,' she explained.

'Aye, lass,' he said irritably. 'First thing they taught me at Oxford was to know when a tart's talking dirty. What I'm trying to work out is, how come you're so keen to fit this randy Eyetie up for murder?'

'Please?'

'Forget it. You're not about to tell me, are you? I see from your file that you were the module pilot?'

'Yes. That surprises you?'

'I stopped being surprised by lady drivers a long time back,' he said. 'And you landed safely? No bumps?'

'No bumps.' She almost smiled.

'Then what?'

'I extended the outside arm to set up the external camera to record this historic moment for posterity. Then Emile activated his TEC and entered the airlock. I opened the exit door and he began to descend. The rest you have seen.'

'Why was he the first out?' asked Dalziel. 'Did you draw lots, or what?'

Now she definitely smiled.

'Certainly we drew lots,' she said. 'Being first is important. Everyone remembers Armstrong, but who can remember the others? Can you, Mr Dalziel?'

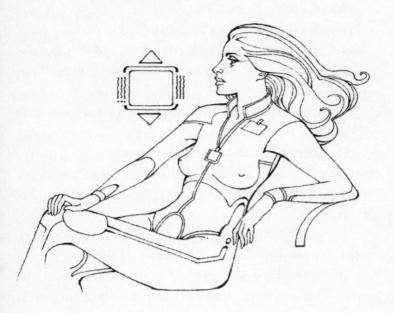

'Nowadays I can't remember to zip me flies till I feel a draught,' said Dalziel. 'Lemarque won when you drew lots, then?'

'Oh no. He did not even bother to take part. He knew it was pointless. Next day the decision came from above. He was chosen. No arguments.'

'Oh aye? How'd they work that out, then?'

She said, 'Who knows? But perhaps you remember from your schooldays, in the playground there was always one little boy or girl who had to have first turn at everything. In Europe that child is France.'

'Was anything said in the module before he left?'

'Only trivial things, I think.'

'My favourites,' said Dalziel.

'Emile said something like, I hope the Yankees have built a McDonald's. Even American coffee must be better than the dishwater we have to drink. Something like that.'

'What do you think he was trying to say before he died?'

She shrugged and said, 'Who can know?'

'*Oh mer* . . . How about, *Oh Marte*?' said Dalziel.

'The vowel sound is not right,' she observed indifferently.

'Dying Frenchman pronouncing a Danish name,' he said. 'What do you want? Professor Higgins?'

She took the reference in her stride and said, 'It would be touching to believe his thoughts turned to me at such a time.'

Touching, thought Dalziel. Aye, mebbe. A hand on the shoulder in an identity parade, *that's* touching!

But he didn't bother to say it. *Or if he pleases through it pass* . . . Silly bugger who wrote the hymn can't have heard of frosted glass, he thought.

V

'You don't look happy,' said Pascoe.

'You do. Found the Paddy amusing, did you?'

'Oh, he's a broth of a boy, sure enough. More froth than a pint of Guinness.'

'Get you anywhere?'

Pascoe said uncertainly, 'I'm not sure, I got a feeling he was trying to manipulate me . . . but you know how Irishmen love to wind up the English. We'll see what you think in the reverse singles. Who do you fancy now. Van der Heyde or Albertosi?'

Dalziel said, 'How come I suddenly get a choice? You made out the list and I'm down for first stab at the Eyetie.'

'Sorry. I got worried in case you thought I was being a bit rigid, pulling rank, that sort of thing.'

'Oh aye? Word of advice,' said Dalziel gravely. 'Pulling rank's like pulling bollocks; once you start, you'd best not let go.'

'Oh aye?' mocked Pascoe. 'You've been at your Rochefoucauld again, I see. Well, one good maxim deserves another. Look before you leap on top of a touchy Italian. Albertosi's psych report says he's got a short fuse. He probably wouldn't have made the trip if the other Italian nominee hadn't fallen off his scooter and cracked his skull. So tread carefully.'

'No need to warn me, lad,' said Dalziel. 'I'm a

53

changed man these days. No more clog dancing. It's all tights and tippie-toe now, believe me!'

'Here's something that'll make you laugh, Marco,' said Dalziel. 'From what's been said so far, you're looking the man most likely to have knocked off Emile Lemarque!'

The Italian's English was nowhere near as good as the two women's, but he had no difficulty with the idiom.

'Who has said this? What have they said?' he demanded angrily.

'General notion seems to be you and him were bonking rivals. You know, jealous of each other's success with the ladies.'

'What? Me jealous of Lemarque? More chance I am jealous of a flea because he bites the woman I love!'

'Flea, you say? You want to watch where you get your women,' said Dalziel kindly. 'But you were both after Silvia Rabal, weren't you?'

'What? Oh yes, he bothers her. Is always flapping round her, calling her his little cockatoo, making jokes. But is all words like with all these Frenchman, talk, talk, talk, so much talk, so little action. Women like men who act, real men, big men. He is no bigger than she is, a midget almost! When a true man comes along, his little cockatoo soon jerks him off the nest!'

Dalziel hid a grin and said, 'So what you're saying

is, Lemarque wasn't worth bothering about, right? But he did bother you, didn't he? So why was that?'

Albertosi grimaced and said, 'You are right. I will not lie. I did not like the Frenchman. But not because of Silvia.'

'Why, then?'

'Because he has a poison tongue! Because he makes slander about me.'

'They're like that, these Frogs,' said Dalziel sympathetically. 'Think yourself lucky you've still got the Alps between you. We've let the buggers build a tunnel so they can come hopping across any time on a day return. What was it he said about you?'

'He said that I have injured my comrade, Giuseppe.'

'Eh?'

'Giuseppe Serena. We are Italy's team for the moon shot, but only one of us will go, it is not yet decided which. Then my friend is riding back to the base on his scooter when a car forces him off the road. He is not badly injured but bad enough to put him out of the running, you understand. Then this pig, this Frenchman, he says it is I who drive the car, I who hurt my friend so that I will be selected!'

It came out in a volcanic rush, flaring (as with Silvia Rabal) into a violent spout of his own language which did not need a dictionary to translate.

'So you wouldn't be too unhappy about Lemarque's death?' said Dalziel.

'What do you say? I am not happy that a colleague

55

dies, does not matter how I feel personally. But, how is it in English?—pride comes, then a fall. He was so boasting he was to be the first to step on the moon. Only he doesn't step, he falls!'

The idea clearly amused him.

'It bothered you, did it? Him getting the prima donna's job?'

'*Prima donna!* That's it! That is how he acts, like he is more important than the others. But what important is it, stepping on the moon? It is more than forty years since Armstrong did it. Since then many more Americans and Russians too. No, this is not a first, not a *real* first.'

'No? What would you reckon is a real first, then?' asked Dalziel.

The Italian smirked knowingly but did not reply.

'All right. Let's stick to facts. You and Silvia Rabal stopped on *Europa* and watched the monitors. Did you see anything unusual?'

This seemed to amuse Albertosi. First he internalized his laughter till his whole body was shaking. Then finally it burst out in a full-throated roar as Dalziel watched, stony-faced.

'Please, I am sorry,' gasped the Italian. 'Go on. Ask your questions. It is reaction, you understand. Much tension, then it comes out in laughter or in anger, makes no matter which.'

'Depends what you're laughing at,' said Dalziel.

'Nothing. Only my foolishness. Go on.'

'All right. Silvia Rabal says that she noticed nothing
unusual on the monitor.'

But he was off again, turning red in his effort to
suppress his amusement.

For a moment Dalziel felt nothing but a school-
teacher's exasperation in the face of a giggling ado-
lescent. Then it began to dawn on him what this was
all about.

'Oh, you dirty sod!' he said slowly. 'That's it, isn't
it? That was *your* first! While Lemarque and the others
were in the module heading for the surface, you and
Silvia were bonking in space. You dirty sod!'

He began to chuckle and a few seconds later his

57

laughter mingled with Albertosi's in a saloon bar chorus. It took the pouring of a couple of large Scotches to calm things down.

'So neither of you was watching the monitor?' said Dalziel.

'When Albertosi makes love, who watches television?' said the Italian complacently.

'And this electrical storm that knackered the transmissions to earth was just a happy coincidence?'

'A slight adjustment of the controls,' smirked Albertosi. 'A man must protect a lady's modesty, hey? Down there these bureaucrats watch us all the time but this they were not going to watch.'

He sipped his drink with a look of ineffable self-congratulation. Dalziel regarded him with an admiring envy which was mainly, though not entirely, assumed. It would be nice to puncture this inflated self-esteem, he thought, but that wasn't the name of the game. The way to a man's mind was through his pleasures.

He leaned forward and said confidentially, 'Just a couple more questions, Marco. First: floating around up there, what was it like?'

vi

'Break for lunch now,' said Pascoe. 'Then we'll have the reverse singles.'

'Fine. How was the Dutchman?'

'Phlegmatic. And the Italian?'

'A bit up in the air,' said Dalziel. And laughed.

The *Europa* crew ate together in their dome, segregated partly by choice, partly by command. Durson had invited Pascoe and Dalziel to join him in the central mess. Conversation stilled for a moment as they entered but quickly resumed.

'So how's it going?' asked Druson.

'Early days,' said Pascoe. 'The crew are naturally eager to get this over and get back to work. Would you have any objection to a limited resumption of duties? It would ease a lot of tension.'

'You mean turn them loose on the surface?' said Druson doubtfully.

'Why not? It's not Jack the Ripper we're dealing with. And there's a hell of a lot of money invested in this programme.'

This appeal to the Great American Motivator just made Druson laugh.

'Hell, they're not going to find anything out there they couldn't read about in our college manuals!'

'Perhaps not,' said Pascoe equably. 'Think about it, anyway. Meanwhile I think at least we ought to have one of our people back on *Europa*. We've tied up your man long enough.'

Again Druson looked doubtful.

Dalziel, who was carving a steak like a Sunday joint, said, 'What's up, Ed? Scared we'll pick the killer and he'll make a run for Mars?'

'Funny. Yeah, OK, why not? Anyone in mind?'

'Rabal, the Spaniard's the obvious choice. She's the pilot. Also, though I've not talked to her myself yet, Andy here reckons she's in the clear and I've never known him wrong.'

You lying bastard! thought Dalziel, chewing on his steak. He got the feeling that Druson for all his street-wisdom was being edged into doing exactly what Pascoe wanted.

'OK,' said the American after a pause for thought. 'Why not? I'll arrange for one of our pods to make the transfer. No need to fuck around with that steam-powered module of yours!'

Dalziel noted the transfer of irritation. You've got the feeling you've been stitched up as well, my lad, he thought. And you've no idea how or why!

Pascoe pushed aside his almost untouched omelette and stood up.

'If you'll excuse me,' he said. 'Couple of things to do. Back to work in, say, fifteen minutes, Andy?'

He just about got the interrogative lift in, dulling the imperative edge of the sentence.

'Whatever you say,' said Dalziel.

They watched him walk away, a slim, upright figure, from behind very little changed from the young detective-sergeant Dalziel had spotted signs of promise in so many years ago.

'Hard man, your boss,' opined Druson. 'And in a hurry. Man in a hurry can make mistakes.'

'Whoever fixed the Frog's suit must have been in a hurry and he didn't make mistakes,' said Dalziel. 'Apart from leaving yon microprobe thing in his locker.'

'Could be even that wasn't a mistake,' said Druson. 'Could be he got instructions to put himself under suspicion and stir things up between the FDR and the French.'

'Oh aye. From which of his masters?' wondered Dalziel.

'From whichever wanted it most,' said Druson. 'I'm just a plain security jock. I don't mess with politics. Now if you'll excuse me, Andy. Anything you want, just ask, OK?'

He's getting worried about the lad wandering around free, thought Dalziel.

He said, 'Aye, there's one thing you could tell me, Ed. What do you lot do about sex up here?'

Back in their dome after lunch Dalziel said, 'Nice guy, Druson. Quite bright too, for a Yank.'

'Indeed,' said Pascoe. 'This afternoon, Andy, let's whip them through at a fair old pace. Don't give

61

them time to think. How does that sound to you as a strategy?'

It was the old Peter Pascoe's voice, easy, friendly, slightly diffident. But running through it now like a filament of high-tensile steel was the unmistakable tone of a man used to giving orders and having them obeyed.

'Sounds fine,' said Dalziel.

He followed Pascoe's instructions to the letter with Kaufmann, hitting him with rapid-fire questions all of which the German handled with the assurance of a man well grounded in the interrogative arts.

'Did you like Lemarque?' he asked finally.

62

'He knew his job, he did his work,' answered the German.

'Aye, but did you like him?'

Kaufmann considered, then said, 'As a man, no. He was like many small men, too aggressive. Always compensating for his lack of height.'

'Give me an example.'

'Well, I recall during training, he found out that O'Meara had been a boxer in his youth, an amateur, you understand. All the time after that, he made jokes about it, pretended to fight with him, challenged him to a bout in the gym.'

'And did O'Meara take up the challenge?'

'Naturally not. Such things would not be allowed. We were training for the mission. Physical injury would have been disastrous for any one of us.'

'So what happened?'

'Nothing,' said Kaufmann. 'O'Meara kept his temper, though I think it was difficult for him sometimes. Eventually Lemarque found a new target.'

'Which was?'

'Me, I think. The Germans in the wars of the last century, something like that.'

'And you kept your temper too?'

'Oh yes. Sometimes I imagined what I would like to do to the troublesome little creature, but it stayed in my imagination.'

'Oh aye. And can you prove that?'

The answer came unhesitatingly.

'All I can say is, if I had decided to kill him, one thing is sure. Everyone would have been quite convinced it was an accident.'

'He had a point,' said Dalziel. 'But not just for him. How come with all their electronic know-how, whoever did it made such a pig's arse of covering their tracks?'

'We've been through this, Andy,' said Pascoe. 'It must have been done in a hell of a hurry. I gather there's only room for one person at a time in the *Europa*'s hold and the TV camera is blocked by the body. So the opportunity's there. But if anyone spent an unusually long time down there, it'd stick out in the recordings at Control, and it doesn't.'

'Aye, well, mebbe I'll get the chance to see what it's like up there for myself before we're done,' growled Dalziel.

'Still thinking we're not following proper procedure?' mocked Pascoe. 'You're such a stickler! It wasn't always like that, I seem to recall. Incidentally, I assume the new Andy Dalziel has been carefully checking out the order they got themselves ready in?'

Dalziel looked uncomfortable and Pascoe allowed himself a superior smile.

'Good news and bad news,' he said. 'The good news is you haven't missed anything by not checking, for the bad news is Lemarque was last into the hold, so it could have been anyone who fixed his suit!'

*

'How does an Irishman get to be an astronaut?' asked Dalziel.

Kevin O'Meara cocked his head on one side in best leprechaun fashion and said, 'Is it an Irish joke you're after telling?'

'Sorry?'

'Do I say, I don't know, and you say, he lights a rocket but doesn't retire till he's sixty-five? Or is it a real question?'

'That's the only sort I know.'

'All right, then. Here's the story of me fascinating life and hard times. I joined the Air Force at sixteen, not out of any sense of patriotism, you understand— *Nor law nor duty made me fight, Nor public men nor cheering crowds*—you'll know your Yeats? No, the only reason I had was to learn to fly so I could become a commercial airline pilot, and make a lot of money, and spend me spare time pleasuring hostesses in palatial hotels. Now isn't that a reasonable ambition for a randy young buck?'

'Sounds fair enough to me,' said Dalziel. 'What happened?'

'I grew up. Or at least I grew older. Young men should be given their heart's desires straight away. If you wait till you've earned them . . .'

He threw back his head and carolled, '*Oh, the youth of the heart and the dew in the morning, you wake and they've left you without any warning.*'

'Don't ring us,' said Dalziel. 'So you just more or

less drifted into the space programme, is that what you're saying?'

'Isn't that the way of most things? You now, I dare say you just drifted into being a policeman.'

'No,' said Dalziel. 'It was what I wanted.'

'Was it now? OK, I'm sorry to hear that. I like my cops to be ordinary chaps like myself who can look at some poor devil in trouble and think: There but for the grace of God go I.'

'If I'd fancied the mercy business, I'd have trained as a nun,' said Dalziel. 'From your file, I see you had a longish period of sick leave about four years back.'

'Is it me file you've got there? Then you'll know more about myself than I'll ever want to know.'

'It was after your wife died, right?'

'Let me think. Yes now, you'll be right. Or was it after the budgie escaped? Drat this memory of mine!'

'Not much to choose between a wife and a budgie, I suppose,' said Dalziel. 'All bright feathers and non-stop twittering. Your missus flew away too, didn't she? Funny, that. You need to be a very cheeky sod to apply for sick leave 'cos the tart who dumped you's got herself killed.'

'That's me all over,' said O'Meara. 'More cheek than Sister Brenda's bum, as the saying is.'

'She'd run off with a Frog, hadn't she?' persisted Dalziel. 'Died with him in a car accident. Terrible bloody drivers, these foreigners.'

'Aha!' said O'Meara. 'At last I'm getting your drift! And here's me thinking you were just showing a friendly interest! Because my wife ran off with a Frog, as you call him, every time I see a Frenchman, I feel an irresistible desire to kill him, is that it? Sure now, it's a fair cop. Except it happens in this case, the Frog she ran off with was a Belgian!'

'Let's not split hairs,' said Dalziel.

'You're right. Many things I am, but not a hair-splitter. Do I get a choice of wearing the cuffs in front or behind? And what happens if I want to go to the little boys' room while I've got them on?'

'You pray no one's been mucking about with your wiring. This sick leave you had, exactly what was it that was supposed to be wrong with you?'

'Oh, women's trouble, you know the kind of thing.'

Dalziel slapped the file down on his knee with a crack that made the Irishman flinch.

'End of happy hour,' he snarled. 'Let's have some straight answers, right?'

'Oh God!' cried the Irishman, clenching his fists in a parody of a boxer's defences. 'You don't mean you're after fighting with the gloves off, is that it? I never could abide bare fists. Bare anything else you care to name, but not the bare fists!'

Dalziel looked at him thoughtfully and said, 'Yes, I'd heard summat about you being a boxer. And about the little Frog taking the piss.'

'Now that's what I call an unfortunate choice of phrase,' said O'Meara.

'I told you, lad. Cut the comedy! Let's just talk about you and Lemarque and the boxing ring, shall we?'

'I thought we agreed to whip this lot through double quick,' said Pascoe irritably.

'Sorry. He bothered me, that one. Something not right.'

'Ah, the famous nose again. What kind of not-rightness?'

'Too many jokey answers and I got the feeling he was trying to steer me around all the time.'

'So what did you end up not getting answers about that you asked questions about?'

Dalziel considered, then said, 'Hard to say exactly. One thing was why he got sick leave after his wife snuffed it, but that can't have owt to do with anything, can it?'

'Unlikely. What was wrong with him, anyway?'

'Don't know. That's the point I'm making,' said Dalziel heavily.

'There should have been a medical report in his file. Hang about, I've still got it here. Sorry. Let's see. Emotional trauma, blah blah; physical symptoms, in-somnia, slight hypertension blah blah; treatment, counselling and unpronounceable drugs; passed fit for duty, 7.10.06. Nothing there that's relevant, I'd say.

Maybe he just doesn't like talking about that time. Stick this in his file, will you?'

Dalziel glanced at the medical report, shrugged and said, 'The bugger's still not right. How'd you do with Danish bacon? Fancy a slice?'

'I don't think so.'

'You don't fancy her or you don't think she's in the frame?'

'I don't think that Miss Schierbeck would judge any man worth killing,' said Pascoe. 'So. One each left. We're not doing too well, Andy.'

'Come on,' said Dalziel. 'You've scuppered the Yanks' motive for Kaufmann being the killer, haven't you?'

'Because he's a double? We knew that before I left earth. It would still be very embarrassing to have to make that public in his defence. No, the only thing that's going to please my masters and cut the ground right from under the Americans' feet is for us to come up with the undeniably genuine perpetrator. There can't be any cover-up or fit-up. We need the real thing and we need it fast!'

After thirty minutes with Adriaan van der Heyde, Dalziel was convinced that either the Dutchman wasn't the real thing or if he was, it would take thumbscrews, rack and Iron Maiden to prise it out of him. He'd heard Pascoe's door open and shut after only ten minutes, signalling that the Commissioner was following his own precept of speed. It annoyed Dalziel to be accused of dragging his feet, annoyed him even more to suspect that perhaps it was age that was making him take so long.

'Look,' he said in desperation, 'let's say you're in the clear, right? Which of the others do you reckon most likely?'

The stolid Dutchman scratched his nose, then said very definitely, 'Albertosi.'

'What?' It occurred to Dalziel that, though it seemed unlikely, it would be nice to pin this on the Italian, not least because Pascoe obviously felt able to dismiss him so quickly.

'Why do you say that?' he asked. 'You reckon mebbe he was jealous of Lemarque?'

'Jealous? Sexually, you mean?' The Dutchman shook his head. 'That's all the British can think of. Sex!'

'Must be something to do with living above sea-level,' said Dalziel. 'All right, tulip. What do you say his motive was?'

'Revenge.'

There was an unnerving certainty about the man's manner and delivery.

Even Dalziel who was not easily impressed by the trappings of honesty couldn't help feeling he had better pay close attention here.

'You'd best explain,' he said.

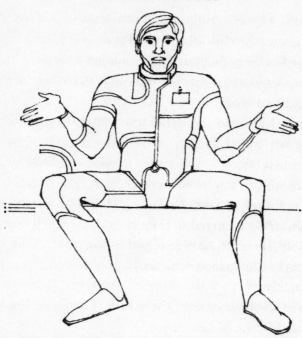

The Dutchman nodded, took a deep breath and began to speak in a measured didactic tone which for a while disguised the incredible content of his allegations.

'Lemarque was approached by a consortium who wanted his help to take over the holy water bottling business in Lourdes. It is a multi-million-franc industry, you understand. He pretended to agree but went to the police. Unfortunately behind this consortium are people who decree that the price of betrayal of their confidence is death. Marco Albertosi was instructed to carry out the sentence.'

For a second Dalziel was reduced to a rare speechlessness. Then he burst out, 'For Christ's sake, are you telling me Albertosi is a Mafia hit man?'

'His family is Sicilian, did you know that?'

'No, I bloody didn't! Come on, lad, where's your hard evidence for all this? For *any* of it!'

'Lemarque's last words. They were incomplete.'

'*Oh mer* . . . So?'

'He was trying to say *Omertà!*' said the Dutchman. 'The Mafia's code of silence.'

For a long moment Dalziel stared into van der Heyde's grave, unyielding face.

Finally he said, 'Are you taking the piss?'

Another long moment, then . . .

'Yes,' said van der Heyde. And his face crazed like an overfired Delft plate into a myriad lines of laughter.

vii

The pod spun round the moon in a climbing orbit and earth swam into view like a schoolroom globe. It was easy for Dalziel to pick out Africa and India, but Yorkshire was invisible under a cloud. He felt a sharp pang of homesickness.

'Long way back, huh?' said Druson, observing him sympathetically.

'Long way to come just to hear a Dutchman crack a joke, right enough,' said Dalziel.

He had rewarded van der Heyde with a glass of Scotch. One glass led to another and he'd finally emerged from the interview with a feeling of childish self-satisfaction at having so blatantly ignored Pascoe's repeated instruction to hurry things along. Logically he had no cause to feel irritated when he found that Pascoe had joined Silvia Rabal in the pod taking her up to *Europa*, but he did. Even the return of Druson with the nightwatch and the message that his 'boss' wanted him up there too didn't mollify him.

'*Boss*'. He couldn't recall the last time he had acknowledged a boss, and he certainly wasn't about to start with a jumped-up detective-sergeant who'd struck lucky!

Mistaking his irritation, Druson said, 'Don't take it to heart, Andy. So the German still looks the man most likely, so what? Let the politicians work it out.'

'Eh? What makes you think I give a toss about politics?'

'You don't?' Druson looked at him shrewdly and said, 'I almost believe you, Andy. So what do you care about?'

'A fair measure in a clean glass,' said Dalziel. 'That'll do me.'

'And Commissioner Pascoe, is that how he feels too?'

'Peter? Straight as a donkey's shaft,' said Dalziel. 'Too honest for his own good sometimes.'

He spoke with a force he didn't quite understand the need for.

'He's done well for an honest man,' observed Druson neutrally. 'But at least he brought you along, so that's a point in his favour, I'd say.'

Dalziel tried to work out the drift of Druson's comments as they came in to dock with *Europa*, but once aboard he needed all his concentration to keep him from bouncing around like a ball in a bingo jar. On the US lunar shuttle he had been safe in the embrace of his wrap-around couch, so this was his first true experience of untrammelled weightlessness. Pascoe watched with open amusement, but Silvia Rabal showed a deal of concern which Dalziel found flattering till he realized she was more worried about her delicate instruments than his delicate body.

Finally, having discovered that the basic art was to reduce his energy output by ninety per cent, he gained sufficient control to follow Pascoe on a tour of the ship.

The fact that every dimension was usable made it feel surprisingly large. There were three main compartments: the bridge, which was the principal control area in the bow; the deck, which was the large central section housing most of the accommodation facilities; and the hold. This was basically a narrow cylinder walled by storage lockers, seven of which had the crew's names stencilled on them.

Dalziel almost filled the central space.

'You'd need to be a bloody contortionist to muck

around with one of them TECs down here,' he said, pulling at the door marked *van der Heyde*. '*Locker*' proved a misnomer. It was held shut only by a magnetic catch and flew open. A framed photo came floating out and he grabbed it.

'These people are highly trained pros,' said Pascoe, behind, or above, or underneath him. 'Also they're very fit and fairly thin. What's that you've got?'

'Family snap,' said Dalziel, passing back a photo of two very plain girls and a scowling woman. 'You can see why he took to space. They're allowed personal stuff, then?'

'Within reason. Weight's not the problem it was.'

'Not for some,' said Dalziel. 'Let's have a shufti.'

He began opening other lockers. This felt more like real police work! But he soon began to feel that these souvenirs of earth were better material for a psychiatrist than a simple bobby.

Surprisingly, only the Dutchman had brought a family photo. Perhaps he didn't trust his memory and was insuring against the shock of reunion. Marco Albertosi obviously felt he could not live without a set of AC Milan's European Cup Programmes. Silvia Rabal's trust in technology did not extend to nourishment and her talisman was a soft leather bag containing sachets of camomile tea and various other pods, seeds, and dried herbs. Dalziel recalled her spicy breath and inhaled deeply. Marte Schierbeck's memento was more mysterious. An old tinder-box. Perhaps she was worried about being marooned? He opened it and found it contained a small tube of contraceptive pills. Perhaps it was who she was marooned with that bothered her! Kaufmann had brought with him a miniature score of Beethoven's *Emperor* concerto. Dalziel marvelled that these squidges could echo as music in some men's minds. Or perhaps it was just a spy's code book after all. The only other book he found was in O'Meara's locker, an ornately bound New Testament with a brass catch.

'Didn't strike me as religious,' observed Dalziel.

'What's that?' said Pascoe.

'New Testament in O'Meara's locker.'

'Oh, you know the priest-ridden Irish. Never shake it off. Bring it out anyway.'

'Hang on. Just one to go.'

It was Lemarque's and it was completely empty. Presumably it had contained nothing except the journal and that had been removed as evidence.

He gave a gentle push and floated backwards out of the hold into the deck area.

'So. One New Testament. Not quite the kind of testament I was hoping for,' said Pascoe glumly.

Dalziel undid the catch and opened the book. On the fly leaf, a book-plate had been stuck headed *Holy Cross Youth Club: Award for service.* Under this was a handwritten inscription *To Kevin (K. O.) O'Meara. Western District featherweight champion, 1993, 1994. Well done!* It was signed, *Father Powell (1 Tim vi, 12).*

'All his success since, and this is what still matters to him!' said Pascoe reflectively.

'You reckon?' said Dalziel, turning to the First Epistle to Timothy.

The page containing Chapter 6 verse 12 was folded in half and when he straightened it out he saw that either deliberately or by chance some flakes of white powder had been trapped there. Some of them floated free. Dalziel licked his finger and stabbed at them, then cautiously put it to his mouth.

'What are you after, Andy? Coke? Forget it. Druggies don't make it on to the space programme, believe me!'

'Why not? They let in spies and killers,' said Dalziel. 'It's not coke anyroad. But I know that taste . . .'

'Probably dandruff. Sorry. All right, pass it here and I'll take it back for analysis just to keep you quiet.'

Dalziel, who didn't think he'd been making any unusually loud fuss, folded the page back to retain the rest of the powder. As he did so he glanced at Verse 12. *Fight the good fight of faith.* No wonder young K. O. O'Meara had won his titles; he'd had the referee in his pocket. His eye strayed a few verses up the column. *For we brought nothing into this world and it is certain we can carry nothing out.* Now there's where Paul had got it wrong. He hadn't given God credit for space travel. Unless, as seemed not improbable, it wasn't a work of God after all.

He fastened the catch and gave Pascoe the book.

The taste was still in his mouth, its source both figuratively and literally on the tip of his tongue.

Druson, who was reclining or hanging on the deck, depending how you looked at it, said, 'You guys gonna be much longer?'

'As long as it takes,' said Pascoe with an authoritative snap which made Dalziel smile and Druson look sour.

'What's in here?' asked Dalziel, examining a couple of doors in the bulkheads.

'Galley and the heads,' said Pascoe.

'Heads?'

'Loos.'

'Oh, the karzies. That's right. You said they just went normal here.'

'Not exactly normal,' said Pascoe, opening a door. 'With no gravity, you need a suction system, otherwise you could be in deep trouble.'

Dalziel examined the apparatus.

'Do yourself a nasty injury with that,' he opined.

He floated above the open door in silence for a while.

'Penny for them,' said Pascoe.

'Still charge a penny, do they,' said Dalziel. 'No, I was just thinking. The Frenchie was so chuffed at being the first to land, and he'd got his little speech ready and all; and he'd not been too long gone from *Europa* where he had summat like a proper bog . . .'

'So?'

'So how come he got so desperate he had to take a

leak on the ladder with the eyes of the universe on him?'

'No one would know,' pointed out Pascoe.

'*He*'d know,' said Dalziel grimly. 'And the data would register on the monitors up here, so they'd know. And then it would be transmitted back to Control on earth so everyone there'd know. And you can bet your bottom dollar someone would leak the leak to the tabloids, so every bugger in the universe would know! So why'd he do it?'

'Stage fright? Or perhaps he drank something. Didn't someone mention something about coffee?'

'Aye. The Dane said he'd been moaning on about how bloody awful it was.'

'There you are, then,' said Pascoe dismissively. 'Coffee's supposed to be pretty diuretic, isn't it?'

And the word switched on a light in Dalziel's lingual memory.

'Bugger me!' he said.

'Why?' said Pascoe with unusual facetiousness.

'That powder in the Testament, I know what it is. It's ground-down Thiabon tablets!'

'You what?'

'*Thiabon*. Trade name for the latest thiazide drug. Quack put me on 'em last year for me blood pressure. They work by releasing sodium from the tissues and stimulating the kidneys to wash it out. In other words, they make you pee!'

'A lot?'

'Worse than draught lager,' said Dalziel. 'In coffee, I reckon they'd have most men going in half an hour. And the build-up's constant. No use crossing your legs. You've got to go!'

'What are you saying, Andy?' asked Pascoe with a frown of concentration.

'No use fixing Lemarque's suit unless you can be sure he's going to trigger the short circuit, is there? So you feed him a diuretic which you know about because you've been prescribed it yourself!'

'Hey,' interposed Druson. 'You're not confessing, are you, Andy? It'll take more than that to get Kaufmann off the hook.'

'No,' said Dalziel. 'But I know someone else who suffered from mild hypertension a while back and could have been put on these pills. Hey, lass. Got a minute?'

Silvia Rabal came down from the bridge. Hair piled up in its comb and wearing a silkily thin leotard in yellow and green, she hovered before them like some tropical bird.

Dalziel said, 'Before word came through that Lemarque was to be first out, who'd won when you drew lots?'

She thought, then said, 'Kevin. But I do not think anyone really believed they would let us decide ourselves . . .'

'Believing the impossible's never bothered the Irish,' said Dalziel. 'So in O'Meara's mind, he should have had the honour of being first out. And beside getting the Freedom of Dublin city and draught Guinness for life, it'd mean money in the bank when it came to writing his memoirs!'

Pascoe was shaking his head, unimpressed.

'It's a pretty feeble motive for killing a man,' he said. 'Now if you were saying it was a daft Irish joke . . .'

'Why not?' exclaimed Dalziel, now in full flow. 'Why not that too? There's nothing he can do about stopping Lemarque, but he can ruin his big moment. If the timing's right, there he'll be, standing on the ladder with all eyes on him, just about to launch into his big speech when suddenly he's got to pee. All right, he may have the nerve to carry *that* off, but not if his suit's been fixed to give him a short sharp shock along the dong? Man'd need to be Christian martyr material not to register that! In fact with a bit of luck, he might even fall off the ladder! Great gag, eh? Only without realizing, O'Meara had fixed it so that all the electronics in the TEC would jam, and the joke goes sour, and the poor bloody Frog is lying dead.'

Pascoe regarded him doubtfully, hopefully, longingly, like a pagan on the brink of conversion, and Dalziel's brain started working overtime, drawing fragile threads together in an effort to plait a cord that would bear the other's soul up to heaven.

'Someone, Kaufmann I think it was, said something about Lemarque twitting O'Meara about being a boxer. Suppose he knew that his nickname as a lad had been KO? Mebbe he'd taken a peek in yon Testament.

81

And suppose what he scribbled in his journal wasn't *Ka is getting angry*, but *Ko is getting angry*. And if he was on the alert, mebbe when he felt his bladder filling up at a suspicious rate, he recalled the awful coffee he'd drunk and knew where to lay the blame. What he said just before he died, *Oh mer . . .* what he was trying to say was *O'Meara!'*

It wasn't much, but a man in search of salvation will make do with a candle if he doesn't get offered a blinding light.

Pascoe said with fervent gratitude, 'Andy, how have I managed without you all this time? I felt there was something about O'Meara when I talked to him. I mentioned it to you, didn't I? Like he was playing a game with me, almost like there was something he wanted me to know . . . Mr Druson, I need to get back to the Village straightaway.'

Druson was looking as if his side's twenty-point lead had been clawed back in the fourth quarter and now in the dying seconds of the game he was watching the opposition shaping to kick a field goal.

'Come on, you guys!' he mocked, trying for time-out. 'I like baloney, but this is ridiculous! Let's just look at the facts here . . .'

'The only fact that need concern you, Colonel, is that we are getting into that pod and that during the flight there will be no talking with your base other than essential technical exchanges. I'm sure you understand me.'

Pascoe's tone was courteous, his voice quiet. But it was the quietness of deep space which can boil a man's blood in millisecs if he challenges it unprotected.

Druson clearly believed he had that protection for now he substituted belligerence for mockery.

'Now listen here. No limey cop gives me orders *anywhere* and especially not round the moon. Christ almighty, it's taken you guys half a century to get here in this junk heap. We've been *living* here for more than—'

Pascoe cut across him like Zorro's sword through a candle.

'Colonel Druson, you are presently on Federation territory and I would be quite within my rights to arrest you and fly the pod back myself with you under restraint. Oh yes, I could do it, believe me. Nor would my powers diminish on the moon's surface, which is by UN accord international territory where my authority is at least equal with that of your own Commander, who, incidentally, has received instructions from your President to extend me all facilities and full cooperation. I hardly think you want to be at the centre of a diplomatic incident which would wipe a mere accidental death right off our television screens. *Do you?*'

Now for the first time Dalziel admitted to himself how far beyond him Pascoe had gone. He'd always known that the sky was the limit for the lad, but somehow, somewhere, a step had been taken which

83

he'd not noticed, a small step which had taken his protégé into territory where not even the mightiest of leaps could have taken Dalziel.

Druson too was taken by surprise, but like Dalziel he was a pragmatist.

'OK, OK, Commissioner,' he said, holding up his hands in mock surrender. 'I'm not taking on the UN, believe me. Down we go, and I'll button my lip all the way, I promise.'

'Thank you,' said Pascoe. 'Andy, perhaps you'd stay here till another pod fetches you. It would be a bit crowded for the three of us, I think.'

He smiled as he spoke, but his eyes flickered to Silvia Rabal and his finger touched his lips. The message was clear. Dalziel was to make sure the Spaniard too made no contact with the village.

Dalziel had seen no particular evidence of the kind of group loyalty which might have her radioing a warning, but Pascoe was right to be cautious. All the same, Dalziel felt a little disgruntled that having done all the nose-work, he wasn't going to be in at the kill.

Still, as Druson had just acknowledged, it was no use kicking against a brick wall. Best to lean back against it and enjoy the sun on your face.

He watched the pod detach itself from *Europa*, then he turned to Silvia Rabal who was relaxing against a bulkhead with her legs tucked up beneath her, looking more like an exotic bird than ever.

'Right, luv,' he said, beaming broadly. 'Now what

can an old vulture like me and a bright little cockatoo like you do to pass the time? With a bit of luck, mebbe we'll get an electrical storm, eh?'

viii

It was the youngster who'd brought the whisky who piloted Dalziel back to the Village. He called Dalziel 'pops' a couple of times, but the fat man was not in the mood to respond and most of the journey passed in silence.

The first person he saw as he climbed from the pod was Druson whose face told him all.

'Seems the Shamrock folded like a zed-bed,' said the Colonel. 'Full admission, signed, sealed and delivered. Just the way you called it, Andy.'

'Oh aye? You might look more pleased,' said Dalziel.

'You too,' said Druson, regarding him shrewdly. 'Time for a snort?'

'Best not,' said Dalziel, to his own surprise as much as the American's. 'I'll need to find out what the lad's planning.'

Druson smiled and said, 'Last I saw of your *lad*, he was talking to the two congressmen and the Air Force general he'd just dumped off the next shuttle. I never heard a guy sound so polite as he says *up yours, fella*!

So it looks like it's goodbye time, Andy. And I guess I'd better chuck in a congratulations. You two are a real class act. Though I'm still not sure if it's Laurel and Hardy or Svengali and Trilby.'

'Is that a compliment?' wondered Dalziel. 'It's about time you buggers learnt to speak plain English. Cheers anyway, Ed. And thanks for the Scotch.'

They shook hands and Dalziel returned to his quarters. Pascoe was already there with his suitcase open on the bed.

'You move quick,' said Dalziel. 'Not like way back when you'd take half a day to make sure a suspect was sitting comfortable.'

'It was like I said, Andy. He was longing to get it off his chest, but it seemed daft to confess when he didn't have to. All it needed was the realization that we had firm evidence. That was down almost entirely to you, Andy. You were brilliant! Fancy a job in the Justice Department?'

'No, thanks,' said Dalziel. 'Good beer doesn't travel. So all's well, eh? No aggro in the Federation after all.'

'The Irish will feel a mite embarrassed but they're used to that,' said Pascoe. 'Main thing is, whatever happens about the Germans, poor Lemarque's unfortunate death won't affect the outcome. It'll be down to honest political debate.'

'Oh aye? What was that thing they taught us about in grammar lessons, when two things are put together that don't make proper sense? Like *freezing fire*. Or *southern beer*.'

'An oxymoron, you mean.'

'Aye, yon's the bugger. Well, honest political debate sounds like one of them to me. And all them as claims they engage in it, I reckon they're oxy-bloody-morons too!'

Pascoe laughed and said, 'You don't change, Andy. Thank God! Come on. Don't hang about. I'm going to have a quick shower. All this frantic activity's made me sweat. You get yourself packed. We're on our way home in half an hour!'

They rose from the moon in a smooth accelerating orbit. As they slipped round for the second time, beneath them they glimpsed the heavy squat bulk of *Europa*, like some beautifully preserved steam engine on display outside a modern jet-station.

Then their flight path straightened out and they sped like a silver arrow towards the gold of Earth.

Dalziel raised himself on his couch. O'Meara was lying to his left, his eyes closed, his breath shallow, a childlike relaxation smoothing the crinkled face.

'Looks as innocent as a newborn baby, doesn't he?' said Pascoe, who occupied the couch to Dalziel's right.

'Aye, he does,' said Dalziel. 'Mebbe that's becaue he is.'

'I'm sorry?'

Dalziel turned to face the younger man and said in an exaggerated whisper, 'Safe to talk now, is it?'

Pascoe thought of looking puzzled, changed his mind, grinned and said, 'Quite safe. Clever of you to spot it.'

'They brought me Glenmorangie,' said Dalziel. 'I'd not mentioned any brand till we got to our rooms and I complained that Druson had forgotten. I checked it out again at lunch. Druson was listening all right. And you knew, but decided not to warn me.'

Pascoe didn't deny it.

'Sorry,' he said. 'Didn't see any point. We weren't going to be saying anything we cared about them hearing, were we?'

Dalziel considered, then said, 'No, lad. We weren't. You because you're a clever bugger and knew they were listening. And me because . . .'

'Because what, Andy?' prompted Pascoe with lively interest.

'Because, not knowing, I'd just come across as a simple old copper doing his job the way he'd always done it.'

'I don't think I'm quite with you,' said Pascoe.

'Oh yes you are. You're only hoping you're not,' said Dalziel. 'Let me spell it out for you, lad. Here's what I think really happened back there. When the Frog snuffed it, the Yanks checked out his TEC. They

88

found a malfunction but no definite sign of outside interference, so it looked like a bug had got into that particular circuit. Tragic accident. Trouble was, the suit was an American design and they don't like looking silly, particularly when they're sweet-talking the Frogs over this Kraut business. So mebbe the first idea was to muck the circuits up a bit to make it look like a maintenance fault, not a design fault. Then someone, Ed Druson most likely, had a better idea. How about setting the French and the Germans at each other's throats by pinning this on Kaufmann? They'd known for some time he'd been spying for the East and had been watching for the best chance to use this info to maximum advantage. A dead Frog blackmailer, a murdering Kraut spy; all they needed was a bit of evidence. So they mucked about with the suit to make the fault look deliberate, planted yon microprobe thing in Kaufmann's locker, leaked the news to the Press, and sat back.'

'And the entry in Lemarque's journal? They forged that too, I suppose?'

'Probably not. Too dangerous. That was just a stroke of luck. God knows what it really means.'

Pascoe leaned back on his couch, shaking his head in a parody of wonder.

'Andy, this is fascinating! Have you been doing a lot of reading in your retirement? Fantasy fiction perhaps?'

'Don't get comic with me, lad,' snarled Dalziel. 'And

don't think you can pull that rank crap you got away with on Druson either. You may be a Federal bloody Commissioner, but me, I'm a private citizen, and I can recollect you telling me more than once in that preachy tone of thine that in England at least being a private citizen outranks any level of public service you care to mention. Or have you changed your mind about that too?'

'No,' said Pascoe quietly. 'I'm sorry. Go on.'

'I was going to, with or without your permission,' observed Dalziel. 'Now your lot, being clever college-educated buggers like yourself, soon sussed out what had really happened, only there was no way to prove it, and even to suggest that the Yanks were fitting Kaufmann up would have caused a huge row with America which nobody wanted. So someone *really* clever came up with the solution—let's accept what the Yanks say about Lemarque's death being deliberate, but let's fit somebody else up instead!'

'And how were we going to manage that, Andy?'

'Well, you had a head start, knowing that Kaufmann had been a double agent, which cut the ground from under the Yanks when it came to motive. But there was still a question of concrete evidence.'

'Concrete? Ah, I see. Like the good old days of slipping half a brick into a suspect's pocket?'

'Oh, you've come a long way from that, Peter,' said Dalziel. 'Anyone can plant a half-brick. Or a New Testament for that matter. But you needed more evidence. You needed an admission, and that requires a long, strong lever.'

'Which I just happened to have about my person?'

'That's where it would have to be, wouldn't it?' said Dalziel. 'I mean, if the Yanks had got us bugged, they'd not be shy about searching our luggage, would they? Though what they'd have made of a harmless list of names and addresses, I'm not sure.'

Pascoe's hand went involuntarily to his breast pocket and Dalziel laughed.

'It's all right, lad. I put it back after I'd taken a shufti while you were in the shower. I knew there had to be something, and it had to be in writing so you could slip it over to O'Meara while you were interrogating him. Then, after giving him time to take this list in, there'd likely be another piece of paper with his instructions on, like, *You're going to confess to killing Emile Lemarque, or else!*'

'Or else what, Andy?' inquired Pascoe. 'You're losing me.'

'Oh, I think I may have done that already,' said Dalziel coldly. 'I can make a stab at guessing what that list meant, but why should I bother when I can get it from the horse's mouth. So how about it, Paddy? I've never known an Irishman keep quiet for so long!'

He poked O'Meara savagely in the ribs and he opened his bright blue eyes and abandoned his pretence of sleep.

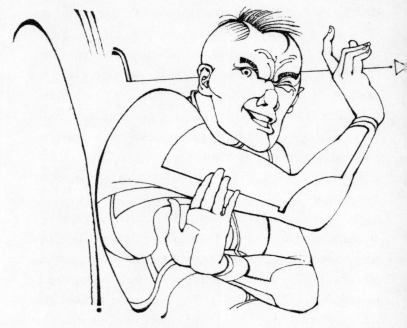

'Now there you are, Andy, me old love,' he said brightly. 'I should have known a man with a face like an old potato couldn't be as thick as he looks! No, no, that's enough of the punching. One thing I learned as a young boxer was not to fight outside me weight. And I got right out of my weight when I was a boy, believe me. Oh, the company I kept, you'd not believe it. Wild men, terrible men, men who drank Brit blood for breakfast and ate Proddy flesh for tea. I was just a messenger, a look-out, a tea-boy, nothing heavy, and I thought I'd put it all behind me when I joined up, and I was glad to be getting away from it all, believe me. But those boys don't forget so easily, and the top

92

and the bottom of it is they came after me to do my old mates a few favours, like giving details of the guard routine at my training depot and looking the other way when I was on sentry so they could get into the arms store.

'Now I was young, but not so young I didn't know that once I started that road, I'd be on it for ever. So, I told our security officer. He was a real gem. He did a deal with the Brits, passing on all information on condition they did the cleaning-up job on their side of the border and pointed the finger a long way from me. A couple of days later, I don't know if it was a cock-up or policy, but the Brits laid an ambush and when the shooting stopped, all the wild men were dead, and me, I was both very guilt-ridden and very relieved, for this meant I was completely in the clear. Or so I thought. Only what I didn't reckon on was that full details of the affair would be carefully recorded in some great computer file where it would lie sleeping for all these years till Prince Charming here came along and woke it with a kiss!'

'He's good at that,' said Dalziel. 'And these names and addresses? They'd be relatives of the men who got killed? And members of your own family?'

'That's right. And if the first lot ever found out who bubbled their menfolk . . . they've got long memories back in Ireland, and they don't forgive. So now you know all about me, Mr Dalziel. And now you know too what nice company you've been keeping.'

Dalziel turned to Pascoe and said, 'Oh Peter, Peter, what have they done to you?'

'Come on, Andy!' protested Pascoe, looking uncomfortable. 'You've cut a hell of a lot of corners in your time, you can't deny it. And we've only got O'Meara's word for it that he turned his old chums in the first time they asked for his help. God knows what mayhem he contributed to before he got cold feet! And what'll happen to him now? He was planning to get out after this mission, we know that. He already has a deal tied up with a publisher, and this will do him no harm at all. An Irish jape that went tragically wrong. End of a promising career with full pension rights guaranteed. Punishment enough from his own conscience, sentence suspended. Advance sales astronomical, serialized in the *Spheroid*, he buys a castle in Killarney and he and his family live happily ever after. I'm practically doing him a favour!'

Dalziel had started shaking his huge head half way through Pascoe's plaintive self-justification, but he didn't speak till it had run its course.

'Oh Pete, Pete,' he said now. 'Christ, but you've started running slow since you've not had me to wind you up! You don't really imagine I'm bothered about this poor Paddy and his tribal troubles, do you? I never met a Mick yet who didn't deserve ten times worse than he got!'

'So why the shaken head, the plummeting sigh, the

heartfelt reproach?' asked Pascoe, trying unsuccess-
fully for lightness.

'Because in all my years of cutting corners, as you
put it,' said Dalziel heavily, 'I did a lot of chancy
things, but I never screwed up a mate. I badgered you,
and I bullied you, and I buggered you about something
rotten. But I never took advantage of you, or made a
dickhead out of you, or fobbed you off with a load of
lies. Did I?'

'Well,' said Pascoe uncertainly, 'there were a couple
of . . .'

'*Did I?*'

'OK, no. In principle, in essence, at the end of the
day, no, you didn't.'

'So why've you done it to me, lad? Why've I spent
the last few days with your hand up my arse working
my jaw-hinges like Charlie McCarthy? Don't answer
that. I'll tell you. It wasn't my sodding expertise and
independence you wanted. With your clout, you could
have had any bright young thing in the game at your
service, spouting your script with a will. But why risk
an act when for no extra cost you can have the real
thing? That would shut the Americans up, eh? Not a
Euro whizzkid out to please daddy, but a genuine
geriatric, out to please no bugger but himself, who
would trip over the truth with his walking frame and
leave the Yanks too bothered and bewildered to cry,
"Foul!" Was it all your plan, Pete? Every bit of it? Or
did some other genius set it off and you just threw me

in as a makeweight to make sure you got your share of the glory?'

His voice never rose above a murmur, but its pace increased and its timbre changed, as waters that start soft and slow become harsh with menace when the meadows give way to rock and the stream starts accelerating towards the cataract.

O'Meara said, 'Oh dear. If you two girls are going to quarrel, I really am going to sleep.'

And sinking back, he closed his eyes once more.

Pascoe too had slumped back into his couch. He did not speak for a long time, then said simply, 'Andy, you're absolutely right. What I did was unforgivable. I don't know how . . .'

His voice failed.

Dalziel said, 'It's a tightrope, lad. The higher you go, the more dangerous it gets. Me, I got as far as I could safely. Beyond that, I didn't fancy the trip. One small step in the wrong direction and you can end up bent, or you can end up using people. People that matter, I mean. Your mates. The other buggers are there to be used, aren't they? Everyone thought I got stuck because them above me didn't care for the colour of my eyes. Bollocks! I could make 'em and I could break 'em. And if I'd wanted . . . but I didn't. Where I was was right for me. Anything more would have been giving a face-lift to a cuddy's backside. But I always thought: There's one bugger I know that I'll trust to go all the way; who'll be able to look up without getting delusions and down without getting giddy; who'll not change to fit changes; who'll not let new honours get more important than old mates . . .'

Now it was his voice that died away.

When Pascoe finally spoke, his voice was tight with restraint.

'Andy, I'm sorry. More sorry than ever I've been about anything. I've let you down and I know it. God knows if I can hope to put things right with you, but I'll try, I promise I'll try. But there's a more pressing problem even than that. I've got to ask you something, not as a friend or even an ex-friend, but as a Federal Justice Commissioner, Andy, you've got knowledge, possibly dangerous knowledge, about O'Meara, about Kaufmann, about the fit-up, about everything.

'Andy, what are you going to do about it?'

What are you going to do about it?

Dalziel rubbed a hand like an eclipse across his face.

This was the second time that day he'd been asked this question.

Then as now he had not given an immediate answer, though he doubted if the delay would have the same result now as then.

His doubts had started long before their arrival on the moon; as soon as Pascoe had telephoned him, in fact. He was no Holmes or Poirot to be hauled out of retirement to solve one last all-baffling case. He was a pensioned-off bobby, suffering from gout, flatulence, distiller's droop, and the monstrous regiment of visiting nurses.

So what the hell was the lad playing at?

He hadn't worked it out straightaway but he'd soon worked out the role Pascoe wanted him to play. The old steam-age detective puffing his way to the pre-ordained terminus! And to start with, he'd really enjoyed playing it. Of course in the old days he'd have done things his way. They'd have visited *Europa* to get the feel of the ship before interrogating the suspects. But his resistance to Pascoe had been token. It was the lad's game, so play to his rules. And the lad had been right. It was pointless planting his clues till he was sure the victim of the fit-up was going to play ball. Mind you, it had been rather offensive the way he'd shovelled them at Dalziel thereafter, as if he really did think his old taskmaster was past it! Best thing that could be said for him was he was working to a timetable. If they hadn't caught this shuttle, they'd have had to wait forty-eight hours for the next, and that would have given the Yanks time to re-group and counter-attack O'Meara with a better offer.

Once Pascoe had got the famous stubby finger to point at the Irishman, all he had to do was get back to the Village as quickly as possible and go through the pre-arranged charade of accusation and confession, with the Yanks listening in helplessly. And preferably without a fat old steam-age cop sitting in the corner, nebbing in with awkward questions.

So the cunning bastard had left him on *Europa*, with the alleged task of making sure Silvia Rabal didn't broadcast anything of what had taken place, this from a ship which was pumping out sound and pictures twenty-four hours of the day!

At this stage he still wasn't sure what was going off. Mebbe Pascoe genuinely believed O'Meara was the perpetrator and had at last learned a lesson Dalziel had once despaired of teaching him, that like faith without works, belief without evidence got you nowhere, so where was the harm in giving God a helping hand?

But it rankled not to be admitted to the plan, if that *was* the plan.

And also, like a stuffed owl, the case against O'Meara *looked* right, but it didn't fly.

With these thoughts in his mind he had watched the pod depart, then turned to look at Silvia Rabal, no stuffed owl this but a living and exotic creature of the air, and matters forensic were flushed from his mind.

'Right, luv,' he said. 'Now what can an old vulture like me and a bright little cockatoo like you do to pass the time? With a bit of luck, mebbe we'll get an electrical storm, eh?'

Even though his tone was nostalgically playful rather than lewdly insinuating, it was not the most gallant of things to say, and had her reaction been scornful abuse, mocking indifference, or even righteous indignation, he would have accepted it as his due. But what rounded those huge dark eyes was surprise; more than surprise, shock; in fact more than shock—fear!

And suddenly, in a flash—but not at all sudden in truth, for this was where the subtle independent micro-circuits of his mind had been directing him while Pascoe was busy with spanner and wrench at the pistons and cogs of his consciousness—he saw the stuffed owl topple off its perch to be replaced by a warm, living, tremulous . . .

'Tell me, luv,' he said. 'What's French for cockatoo?'

She went floating away up into the bridge, fluttering her supple hands over the bank of control lights, and for a moment both terrifying and exhilarating he thought she might be going to send them blasting off into the depths of space.

But then she turned and floated back to face him.

She said, '*Kakatoès*. He called me Ka when we were . . . in private. But you know this, and more. Not everything perhaps. But enough to guess everything. From the start I saw you were the dangerous one.'

She spoke almost flatteringly. She was also speaking unnecessarily freely considering all those TV cameras.

He said warningly, 'Mebbe we should . . .' What? There was nowhere private to go! But she took his meaning and laughed, making a flapping gesture with her hands.

'It is all right. No witnesses. These electrical storms are sometimes convenient, hey?'

'You mean you've fixed it?' A light dawned. 'Of

course, it was you who fixed it last time, not Marco. It was *your* idea.'

'Of course. I guessed Marco might boast, but he's too macho to tell it was not his initiative!'

'Why'd you need to do it?'

'I often imagined how it might be in zero gravity,' she said mischievously.

'I meant the blackout.' He frowned.

'Oh, that. If Control had spotted a fault in Emile's TEC circuits during the module descent, they might have aborted the landing and spoilt my plan.'

She was bloody cool, thought Dalziel. Another thought occurred to him and he said, 'But weren't the suits tested earlier in the voyage out?'

'Of those involved in the landing, yes.'

She regarded him expectantly. It was as if she wanted him to justify her decision to black out the cameras and confront him directly. Though what she hoped to gain by that . . .

As often happens with sight, taking his eye off a sought-after object brought it into view.

He said, 'I saw the files. You and Lemarque are the same height, so your suits would be much the same. You fixed your suit at your leisure, didn't you? You had time to do a real job on it, not this botched-up job the Yanks claimed. Then all you had to do was swap the suits. And the name strips, That's why his was out of line. You had to do that in a hurry down in the hold. I should have remembered the smell.'

101

'Smell?'

'In Lemarque's suit. That spicy smell. I thought it were a funny kind of aftershave . . .'

And now the memory of her spiced breath and the contents of the leather pouch in her locker came together and he said, 'What was it you put in his coffee to make him pee? Dandelion juice? Used to call them piss-the-beds when I were a lad.'

'Dandelion, pansy, burdock, black briony—just a very little of the briony, it is very poisonous, very dangerous to those who do not know how to use it. When I hear he is dead, at first I thought: My God, I have used too much and killed him!'

Her face paled with the memory of shock. Dalziel scratched his nose reflectively and said, 'Aye, but you *did* kill him, lass.'

'No!' she protested indignantly. 'He dies by accident! All I do is give him a shock, make him ridiculous in front of the whole world! You must believe me, Dalziel. You must!'

She looked at him beseechingly and he said, 'Must I? I'll need to know a lot more before I can go along with that. First thing I need to know is why you wanted to electrify his goolies anyway.'

She scowled and said, 'He was a rat! He turned from me to that Danish icicle. Well, that was his right. I grow tired of men too. But this rat wanted us both, he is insatiable. Even that I don't mind. But he hid it from me and he did not hide it from her, and that I mind very much! She knew I was being tricked and found it amusing. They screw with their minds, these Scands. But it was his fault, so I decided he must be punished and this idea came. It seemed to me—what is your phrase? Poetical justice! That's it. To pain him in the places he valued most. His vanity and his sex! But pain only, not death. You cannot laugh at a dead man, can you?'

This sounded like a clinching argument to Dalziel.

'So you're saying it was a fault in the TEC design that killed him? But if you hadn't interfered with it, that fault would never have shown up.'

'My interference was a possible fault, therefore it could occur, so this other fault was the real fault,' she flashed.

'Mebbe that makes sense in Spanish,' he said. 'So you definitely left it looking like an accidental fault?'

'Of course! You think I am stupid?' she cried. 'So what has happened? How is it you are looking for a killer? And why is Kevin accused? How can that idiot who comes with you believe such a stupidity? Kevin will prove his innocence, won't he?'

He missed the implication of this for the moment as his mind tried to rearrange everything he knew into something he could understand. And as the picture emerged like a negative in developing fluid, his slab-like face grew cold and hard as a rock on a wintry fell.

'I'd not put money on it, luv,' he said. 'In fact, I'd bet that yon idiot who comes with me has probably

got O'Meara's full and frank confession in his pocket
already.'

'Confession? Why should he confess?'

'I don't know yet. But one thing's for sure. Somehow
it'll seem a better option for him than not confessing.'

She digested this.

'You think so? Then in fact, I will be helping Kevin
by keeping quiet, is that not so?'

He grinned at her ingenuity, and also at her naïvety.

'Bit late to be thinking of keeping quiet when you've
just coughed your guts out to me, luv,' he said cheer-
fully.

'Coughed? Oh yes. I understand.' She smiled at him
with wide-eyed innocence. 'But I do not understand
why you say I have coughed? There is no one here. Just
you and me and the electrical storm. No witnesses.'

She gestured at the useless TV eyes.

Dalziel shook his head and showed his gums in a
chimpanzee's smile.

'Good try, luv,' he said. 'But they don't like us using
a notebook and a stubby pencil any more.'

From his breast pocket he took a flat black plastic
case with a silver grille along one edge, held it up to
his ear, pressed a button and listened to the resulting
faint hiss with every appearance of satisfaction.

'That's grand,' he said switching off. 'I was a bit
worried in case the electrical storm had affected the
recording quality.'

She stared at him, baffled, unsure, as he replaced

104

the instrument in his pocket. He met her stare full on, raised his eyebrows as if to invite her comment. She moistened her lips nervously. At least it started as nervousness, but the tiny pink tongue flickering round the full red lips carried a sensual jolt like an electric shock, and when she saw his reaction, she smiled and let the tongue slowly repeat the soft moist orbit.

And then it was he heard that question for the first time.

'So, tell me, Dalziel,' she said. 'What are you going to do about it?'

They were facing each other across the desk, resting against the bulkheads. If there was an *up* and a *down* on the *Europa*, this configuration came closest to what Dalziel thought of as 'standing up'. Perhaps that's what made him take the step.

One small step.

Indeed, hardly that. On earth it would have been a mere shuffling of the feet, a rather nervous adjustment of a man's weight as he wondered what the hell to do next.

Only here there was no weight to adjust, and the small forward movement of the left foot provoked a counterbalancing backward movement of the right; and as this was against the bulkhead, it caused an equal and opposite reaction, thus doubling his forward movement; and now his arms swung back to grab for support, but, finding nothing to get hold of, merely struck hard against the surface, and this energy too was translated into forward momentum.

And so it was that one small step for Dalziel became in a split second a mighty leap.

She came to meet him. In her eyes a deal had been offered and enthusiastically accepted, and she was no niggard in a bargain. There was perhaps a moment when she became aware that the thin black plastic device spinning in the asteroid belt of clothing that soon surrounded them was not a recorder but an electric razor, but by then it was far too late to abort the blast-off. Far too late . . . far, far too late . . .

*

106

'Andy? *Andy!* Are you OK?'

'What? Oh aye. Sorry. What was it you said?'

'I thought we'd lost you there,' said Pascoe. 'I asked you: What are you going to do about it?'

Dalziel regarded Pascoe with the exasperated affection he had bestowed on him almost from their first encounter. He'd thought then that mebbe the bugger was too clever for his own good, and now he'd got the firm evidence. The lad had sat down and worked out everything, method, motive, the lot. Jealous resentment, a jape that went wrong, the use of a diuretic in the coffee, everything had been there in his theoretical model. Only, that was all it had been to Pascoe. A model theatre into which he could dangle his puppets and watch them dance as he pulled their strings. He hadn't been able to take the next small step and see that if a model works, then mebbe the reality works too, and perhaps there was no need of puppets, because there was a real culprit out there, waiting to be caught.

And because he was so obsessed by clever trickery, he had thought to authenticate it all by dropping fat old Andy Dalziel into the play, a figure so obviously real that not even the suspicious and distrustful Druson could believe he was anyone's puppet.

So what *was* he going to do? In a way, the ultimate disappointment was that the lad needed to ask. Dalziel didn't believe in practising everything he preached, but the golden rule he'd recently reproached Pascoe with was twenty-two carat. You don't drop your mates in it.

And anyway, whether he'd intended it or not, a deal had been struck back there on *Europa*.

'Do?' he growled. 'What can I do? You're in with the dirty tricks mob now, lad, and I don't want to end my days with a poisoned umbrella up my gunga!'

'Andy, you don't really believe that?' protested Pascoe. 'No threats. It's what you think right that matters.'

'I think it right to go on living as long as I can,' said Dalziel. 'All right, all right. For Christ's sake, take that hang-dog look off your face before the RSPCA puts you down. I'll keep stumm. And I'll forgive you. It's my own fault, I suppose. Teach a fledgling to fly and you've got to expect he'll crap on you some day. But I'm not going to kiss and make up, if that's what you're after!'

Pascoe's face split in a smile of undisguised, uncontrived relief.

'I should have known better than to mess around with you, Andy,' he said. 'I thought . . . well, to tell the truth, I thought you'd be so rusty, I wouldn't have any bother. And I wanted to see you again, and to work with you. Honestly, that was part of it. But I underestimated that nose of yours. It must be the weightlessness that got it back working at full power.'

'Not just the nose,' muttered Dalziel.

'Sorry?'

'Nowt. Summat I meant to ask. *Europa*, it doesn't just mean Europe, does it?'

'No. It's the name of a Phoenician princess who got ravished by Zeus in the form of a bull.'

'Oh aye. I thought I recollected something like that,' said Dalziel with a certain complacency.

Pascoe turned his head to look back to the moon. They were far too distant now to see the orbiting spaceship, and the moon itself had declined from a world to a silver apple hanging in space.

'I can't believe I've really been there,' he said dreamily. 'I used to look up at it when I was a kid and have these fantasies. Now I'll be able to look up and remember . . . but I doubt if I'll believe what I remember. What about you, Andy?'

'Oh, I'll believe right enough,' said Dalziel, who was lying back with his eyes shut, thinking of Nurse Montague and a nice little surprise he might be bringing home for her. 'Like yon Yank said, one small step for a man, one mighty jump for an old copper.'

'Leap.'

'Eh?'

'*Leap*,' repeated Pascoe with that stern pedantry which neither age nor advancement had been able to rid him of. 'I think you'll find it was *one giant leap*, not *one mighty jump*.'

'You speak for yourself, lad,' said Andrew Dalziel.

THE END